Shadow

of the

Blue Ridge

Cyberworld Publishing established 2009

www.cyberworldpublishing.com

Cyberworld Publishing
Jindalee St
Toronto, 2283 NSW
Australia

Shadow of the Blue Ridge

Gary D. Kessler

Table of Contents

Introduction	7
Fire on Ice	10
Bouncing Back	21
Joleen Finds Her Voice	26
The Invisibles	36
Converging Divergence	45
The Passing of Little Eddie	49
Thanks Rosa	53
The Photograph	56
What to Do with Rusty	65
Timing Out	70
Molly's Picnic Table	76
How Big the Ocean?	85
Good Customer	91
The Present	97
Just Two More Years	104
Poison Pen	114
A Place at the Table	123
A Question of Wisdom	128
Mothers' Lament	136
Where's Karen?	141
False Flight	147
The Last Word	156
Overdue	164
Bill-'N-Bob	169
Last Treasures	174
Second Mom	180
Awards and Credits	189
About the Author	191

Introduction

Despite having traveled all over the world in the last fifty years, with extended residences in Japan, Thailand, and Cyprus, I kept coming back, in person and imagination, to the Blue Ridge Mountains of Virginia. My wife and I met in Charlottesville, where we both attended the University of Virginia, and then, although we drifted off in foreign service assignments with the U.S. government, we didn't leave before buying our own slice of paradise in the Piedmont foothills of the Blue Ridge and returning to the region again and again until finally retiring there. The twenty-six stories in this collection, written over a fifteen-year period, are all set within sight of either side of this range of mountains, and extending from Front Royal in the north to Roanoke in the south.

I had written six novels of espionage and intrigue set in the Mediterranean before retiring from my first career and beginning another one as a freelance mainstream publishers' book editor in the shadow of the Blue Ridge. I first began writing short stories for regional competitions, encouraged by placing with more than half of what I was writing and having the rest judged to be good enough to be published in anthologies. Taking my inspiration from the vibrant and teeming-with-life Charlottesville Downtown Mall, this bricked-over main street became the subject of my first published short story collection, *On the Downtown Mall*. This anthology unfolds the interlocking stories of people traversing the Charlottesville Downtown Mall throughout a day in April, moving from the western end of the mall to the eastern end. The eastern end is now anchored with an entertainment pavilion that wasn't there when the book was written, but the Mall of the imagination did include a children's carousel, the focus of one of my short stories, that was only added to the Mall after the book was published. Since the publication of that anthology I have continued spinning out stories set in the shadow of the Blue Ridge for competitions and other anthologies.

The inspirations for the stories in this collection are varied. The first, "Fire on Ice," and the last, "Second Mom," were born over the dinner table in conversations with friends about their experiences. The "nubs" for stories, such as "The Present," "Bouncing Back," and "Last Treasures," were gleaned from family legends. Some, including "False Flight," "The Invisibles," "Molly's Picnic Table," "Thanks Rosa," and "How Big the Ocean?" were snatched from news media headlines. Two, "Converging Divergence" and "The Passing of Little Eddie," were inspired by art images. A few, such as "Good Customer" and "Just Two More Years," incorporate elements of the lives of neighbors. "Poison Pen," "A Place at the Table," "A Question of Wisdom," "Mother's Lament," and "Where's Karen?" were all written from biblical references. But the overarching inspiration of all of the stories in *Shadow of the Blue Ridge*, as written in their current form, is just that—they all are set in the shadow of one of the oldest and most accessible mountain chains in the world.

All of these stories have been gleaned from published anthologies. The first two thirds of the stories in the collection were entries in various regional writing contests— the sadly now-demised annual *HooK* short story contest, judged by the novelist John Grisham; the annual art-based writing contest, the Writer's Eye, sponsored by the University of Virginia's Fralin Museum of Art; and the Virginia Writers Club annual competitions, conducted through its regional chapter, the Blue Ridge Writers.

More than half of these stories first appeared in the *Blue Ridge Anthology*, *Skyline*, and *Writer's Eye* anthologies. Four were first published in *On the Downtown Mall*: "How Big the Ocean?," "Good Customer," "The Present," and "Just Two More Years."

Five stories were taken from a Bible study collection, *(Re)Tell Me the Stories*, coauthored with my minister sister, Carole Stockberger, and formulated from discussions on the perplexity of selected Bible stories with our mother in the last year of her life. The stories representing this collection here are "Poison Pen," "A Place at the Table," "A Question of Wisdom," "Mother's Lament," and "Where's Karen?"

"False Flight," lifted from one of my pen name anthologies, *Final Flight* by Olivia Stowe, is one of eight stories providing a possible scenario for a mysterious plane crash in the Blue Ridge in 1963. Three of the stories, a combined exploration of the concept of nearly lost opportunities, "Overdue," "Bill-'N-Bob," and "Last Treasures," were originally published in *The WritersNet Anthology of Prose*.

There has been no end to the creative inspiration that living in the shadow of the Blue Ridge Mountains has provided me. I have thoroughly enjoyed writing in the setting of this slice of heaven. I hope you enjoy reading these stories as much as I enjoyed writing them.

Gary D. Kessler
Charlottesville, Virginia
September, 2015

Fire on Ice

Please, God, this isn't happening. Where did I go wrong? What did I do wrong? When did this dusting of snow become deep drifts?

We were struggling along the trail—or at least I hoped we were still on the Appalachian Trail. Two scouts and me. But it was hopeless. It was quite dark now. What we'd said was that if any of the teams of boys didn't return to the Hump Back Rock parking lot at the end of two hours, we'd send searchers for them. They were to stay on the trail and in their designated sector. We'd come along the trail, blowing our whistles, and then we'd be sure to meet up. No problem.

It was a simple compass direction-finding exercise. We'd done it here for years and never had a problem. Where did I go wrong this time?

Who could have guessed it would get so dark so fast, or that the snow would roll in like this? This afternoon it had been quiet along the trail. Now the wind was howling. There was no way the boys could hear us whistle. The wind took the sound completely away. Was this what fear sounded like? The whistles were hopeless. But we still whistled as we trudged the trail—if we were still on the trail. With the snowfall it was so hard to tell. What else could we do but whistle? It seemed such a simple and effective plan.

I turned my eyes on Brian and Chris. They looked as cold and frightened as I was. I couldn't show it, though. I was the scout master. They trusted me.

"Tell you what, boys. The wind is too loud for the whistles. I think we should go back to the others now and move over to the visitor center. It will be warmer there."

"But Doug and Shawn and Paul are out here somewhere," Brian said, having almost to yell over the moaning of the wind through the trees.

As if I didn't know that.

"I think it's time we got some help," I said. "Come on, boys; we need to turn back."

I tried to sound calm. Not to let the hysteria show in my voice. Three boys. Doug Wilson and Shawn Peters . . . and Paul Singleton. They were real. All of them were somebody's son. And I was responsible for them.

Oh, God. Let me wake up. Let this be a dream. Three boys. All somebody's son. Paul my own son.

Yes, Brian, I damn well do know how hard it is to turn back. But you are my responsibility too.

Only one car at the parking area.

"They've already gone over to the visitors' center," a grim-faced Al Jones, assistant club master, said. "Travis thought we'd better call it in. You were gone too long."

The visitor's center was still deserted when we gathered over there. I'd left Al at the parking area—just in case the boys turned up there. Travis had used the emergency telephone on the center's porch.

The wind wasn't too bad at the visitor's center. More than once I told myself to get back out onto the trail—that the wind had calmed down. But the whipping of the tops of the trees told me differently. We were just protected here. God, I thought, I hope the boys remember how to hunker down. What had we studied so far in survival training? So many years, so many boys. I couldn't remember what we'd covered this year. Paul was a senior scout. I'd put him with Doug and Shawn on purpose—a steadying influence. Both of them sort of smartasses. Should I have set the groups up differently?

I heard the sirens from a long distance. If I could hear the sirens, why couldn't we hear the whistles on the trail? Sirens coming from both ends of the parkway. The world gone angry, whirling red.

Help had arrived. It should have lifted responsibility from my shoulders. But, of course, it didn't. These were my boys. Paul was my own son. Lots of help. Too much help.

"We're where three counties meet," Travis responded to my look of confusion. "Three sheriffs' departments. And the Park Service too."

I went, frantically, from one to the other as they milled around, talking jurisdiction and organization,

11

compartmentalizing the search grid, discovering their communications systems didn't match. Talking, posturing, getting nowhere.

Another vehicle approaching. A van, with antennas on top. The media.

I reached for the cell phone. It was time to call the families. They shouldn't first learn of this on the TV news. The hardest call was the last one.

"You're late. We held dinner for you for a while, but Cindy was getting hungry, so we went ahead and ate."

"There's a problem, Margaret."

At the end of a highly emotional exchange, Margaret said in that determined voice of hers, "I'll find someone to sit with Cindy and I'm coming up there."

"Please don't. Cindy shouldn't be alone, and people will be calling to the house. There's nothing you can do here. You can help best right where you are. They . . . they have it all under control."

I almost couldn't get that last sentence out. I didn't want Margaret to know how much under control they didn't have it. But who was I to judge or complain? They had come out on a cold, snowy night to find my son—the son I had lost.

But, at last, one of the sheriffs had asserted himself. I was panicked when I saw which one, though. An old Marine. No kids. The other two sheriffs had young sons. That meant a lot to me right now. I built up the courage to approach the sheriff after, at last, he'd organized and dispatched search parties.

"Don't they have airplanes or helicopters for this sort of thing? We tell our boys to look for them in case of trouble. They know how to signal."

"Can't. Too windy. Not much to see at night anyway," he answered—rather abruptly, I thought. But of course he was right.

He hadn't even looked at me. He knew who to blame for this too.

At that moment Shawn Peter's parents pulled up in their SUV. Ed Peters made a beeline for me, his wife, in

12

curlers, dragging him down with a grip on his arm, yelling for him to calm down, she almost in hysterics herself. I braced for the onslaught. Ed Peters was quicker to find fault than to pitch in and help. And he had a lot of fault to find in me right at this moment.

I hadn't gotten hold of Doug's parents yet. He was supposed to spend the night with us after this scout outing. I assumed they were out partying, given the free night. God, I hoped whatever bar they were in didn't have a TV.

* * * *

"Hey, look. I can see a big pond down there in a fold between the hills."

"Yeah, it looks frozen," Shawn said. "I wonder how deep it is—and how thick the ice is."

"Don't know," Paul answered. "But it's about time for us to turn back. We must be almost out of the sector we were assigned, and we've only got three-quarters of an hour to get back to the rendezvous point." Paul gave a long, lingering look toward the pond, though. He could remember going skating without skates on the pond on his granddad's farm.

"Last one down gets cleanup duty at the next den meeting," cried out Doug as he took off down slope through the trees.

The other two boys raced after him, laughing.

* * * *

I'll never forget the smell of varnished old pine. It will forever conjure up what the sheriff said when he thought I was asleep—or I certainly hope he thought I was asleep. I was curled up on the floor of the visitor's center, exhausted and unable to sleep I was so keyed up. At the same time I had my eyes scrunched closed, trying to shut out reality and providing an excuse not to be here, the last place I wanted to be.

Ed Peters was perched on a straight chair over near the center's book rack, the essence of a rumbling volcano,

13

ready to erupt at the slightest excuse. His eyes were boring into me. His wife was ineffectually fluttering around, trying to be domestic with no means to do so or anyone interested in being thus served—but obviously trying to maintain a claw hold on her role in life.

I had sent Al and Travis down the mountain with the remaining scouts—the ones whose parents hadn't already driven up here and snatched them away. They would make sure the boys got home, with explanations—sort of a hollow gesture of responsibility, I painfully knew. And afterward Travis would try to find Doug's parents. I didn't envy him that.

I knew we'd already been on the 11:00 p.m. news. By then there were two film crews up here and both did live segments. They wanted me on film, but the sheriff in charge insisted that only he be interviewed—and that was fine with me. I never could understand how the relatives of the victimized or lost could speak on camera. I knew I wouldn't do more than cry. And *that* certainly would bolster everyone's confidence.

I must assume the sheriff thought I was asleep when he turned to a colleague of one of the other counties and said, sotto voce, out of Ed Peters' hearing, "It's almost 3:00 a.m. It's getting too dangerous out there. It's time to turn off the search for tonight and come back tomorrow to look for the bodies."

I section my life into two segments—the years before I heard that statement, which was a period in my life during which I only thought I endured problems and grief but that really were the innocent years, and all of the years after I heard the sheriff say that, when I knew how precious and fleeting life and happiness were. I felt a fist grip my heart and squeeze, and I could barely breathe. Even my moan was too strangled to be heard.

I was rent asunder. Emotionally I knew that I should reach out in concern for the parents of Shawn and Doug, but in those moments I was so overwhelmed with the terror and grief of this sentence so casually and callously inflicted on my own son—all because of what I had failed to do—that I

14

could think of no one but my own Paul. I even, I am mortified to think, resented Ed Peters at that moment. He had more time than I did. Maybe merely moments before he realized that the sheriff was shutting down the operation. But precious moments of innocence and hope that I no longer had.

I closed my eyes even tighter, willing them all to leave. All of them just to pack up and drive off, knowing that as soon as I was alone, I would bundle up once more and be out on that trail. I knew what that inevitably meant. And in my grief and frustration and deep sense of guilt, I embraced it.

* * * *

"Be careful, Shawn. That section of ice looks too thin to hold you."

"Didn't even see it. It's too dark," Shawn answered.

All three boys looked up to the sky at the same time, as if just now, in consort, awakening from a deep sleep. It was dark and snow was beginning to fall. And it was cold and the wind was picking up.

"Shit, we're late for the rendezvous," Paul declared, having looked at his watch.

"Better get back on the trail pronto," Doug said, working his way to the edge of the pond.

Once off the ice of the pond, the three turned in separate directions.

"Which way to the trail?" Shawn asked.

"Should be to the west of us," Paul said. "Whichever way the sun went down."

"You see the sun go down? I didn't see the sun go down." It was Doug who said this, but it could have been any of the three of them.

"Uphill?" Shawn offered.

"Which uphill?" Paul snorted. "We're in almost a hollow. It's uphill on three sides."

"The downhill side must be east then," said Shawn, trying to keep logic going.

15

"Maybe," Paul answered. "But you can't tell in the Blue Ridge. Can we be sure which side of the ridge we're on?"

"We can use the compass. That's what we came out here to practice."

Shawn and Paul turned and gave Doug a sharp look. It was the most intelligent thing he'd said this school year. But then no one spoke up to claim having the compass, and the three shared gazes of disgust and the beginnings of fear.

"Three hills. Three of us. We should each take a hill, and whoever finds the trail can give a shout." This time Shawn's less-than-brilliant idea.

"I'm already shouting and you can barely hear me four feet away," Paul countered. "The wind. It really moans on the mountaintops. And, no . . . basic survival. What my dad taught us. We stay together and we stay in one place. Someone has to come for us if we're getting out of here tonight. Tomorrow we can be more adventuresome."

"I'm cold. And it's snowing," Shawn whined.

"Branches. You gather branches, Shawn. And, Doug, you look for a good sheltered spot. All of us should stay within sight of each other, though. Build down low, in a small ravine, away from the direction of the wind, if we can decide what's prevailing. I'll build a fire."

"Not here," Doug said. "Your dad warned us how easy a forest fire could start in a dry winter like this."

Once more looks of surprise and just a bit more respect went Doug's way from the other two. He'd remembered what they hadn't.

"Then we'll build it out on the pond. On the ice," Paul answered, a sense of determination in his voice and surprising even himself that he had come up with this solution. They needed to stay calm. And they needed a leader. Paul knew this is why his dad had spent all this time in scouting with him—to make him a leader in trouble like this. "If anyone's going to find us tonight, it will be because we gave them a signal location."

"Won't it just melt through the ice?" Shawn asked.

"Yes. And then we'll build another one, if we have to. We'll take turns. We each have our poncho. We'll huddle together for warmth in whatever shelter we can put together. We'll take turns being in the middle, and when the fire goes out, that's the guy who's got to go out and start another one. Food and water. My canteen's pretty full. Yours?"

Both of the other boys wagged their heads to indicate that they had enough for now.

"And food?" Both Paul's and Doug's heads swiveled toward Shawn, the food-obsessed of the three of them.

"You know I'm loaded with candy bars," he said. "You laughed at me down in the parking lot for what I was bringing."

"OK, go, go, go. Let's get under cover."

* * * *

Margaret almost didn't answer the telephone. She was exhausted by the number of calls she was getting from friends and relatives—and complete strangers. All wanted to do anything they could to help. Two calls before, with a tearing heart, she had turned down an offer of help from a retired forest ranger. Ralph went to their church, and he recalled to Margaret that her husband had paid a house call on a stormy night and had doctored and stayed with his daughter until her fever broke and probably had saved her life.

"You say the word, Margaret, and we'll go up there. I've gotten in touch with a group of other retired forestry service rangers. We know that area like the back of our hands."

"They have more than enough help, Ralph. Thanks. But thanks. And, yes, I'll let Matt know you offered and are ready."

The selfish part of her had wanted to answer, "Yes, put as many people out there looking for my precious son as will go." But she knew this wasn't a night for a seventy-five-year-old man to be on the mountain in the woods in a snowstorm, no matter how well he knew the area. She could

17

not conscience the risk of trading one life for another. Even her son's. But she felt so powerless—and useless.

And on the next call, her world shattered.

"They're calling off the search for the night, honey. The Albemarle sheriff is driving me home now. They dragged me out. Wouldn't let me stay up there."

The last thing Margaret said to him before he clicked off was, "Matt, it's not your fault." She wouldn't have said it if she didn't believe it. Everything didn't have to be someone's fault. She knew that everything Matt had been doing for years was to prepare young men for something like this—to teach them how to survive it. No matter what, she knew she had to convince Matt that this wasn't his fault.

She let the phone ring five times before answering it next. She had sunk to the floor beside the telephone from the body blow of Matt's call. She didn't know if she could take any more of this.

"Margaret?"

"Steve?" She recognized the voice instantly even though they hadn't spoken in months. She couldn't even remember now what the falling out with her brother had been about. But, as she remembered it, it was too serious and too much Steve's fault, she believed, for her to make the first move.

"I got a call from the guys on duty over at the Nellysford firehouse. They say they've seen the pinpoint of a fire on the mountain. To the north of Wintergreen."

"A fire? On the mountain?" Margaret felt like a dope. She didn't know what that meant. The mountain was on fire? She knew they were in a heavy risk period. Everyone on the slopes of the Blue Ridge knew that. And a call from the Nellysford firehouse? How in the hell could Steve expect her to care about a forest fire at a time like this?

"I understand that's the area those boys should be in," Steve continued. "The guys say the light comes and goes—but they have it pinpointed. I'm on my way to the firehouse, and we're going up there on a fire trail the guys know about."

"They've called off the search for the night," Margaret said dully. "The sheriffs have ordered everyone off the mountain." Everything about her felt like it was paralyzed, shutting down. She could barely get her words out. Her mouth felt like it was full of cotton.

"Fine for them. But I haven't called any search off. It's our county up there, and it's a fire. And . . . and Paul's my nephew and you're my sister."

* * * *

The boys first saw the lights of the flashlights across the pond, downhill. They had just decided that someone had to go back out on the ice and make another fire, but, without saying it, each had pretty much given up on that idea. And it was so cold, even huddled together like that. It wasn't so much of either an adventure or fun anymore as they had been pretending it was.

Doug saw the lights first, and Paul told him that he was just hallucinating. If help was going to come, it should come down from the Appalachian Trail, not up the mountainside. But then Shawn said he saw the lights too. So they groggily and painfully stood up from their huddled crouch and stumbled out of their improvised shelter. They each instinctively knew if they didn't and if it was a search party, it easily could just pass them by.

It had been Doug who suggested that at least one of them had to be awake at all times. Paul didn't remember having read that in any of his survival manuals and he'd given lip to Doug about it, but Doug had stood his ground.

"I didn't read it in the manuals either. Your dad told us that," Doug said indignantly.

Doug had always been the dopey and smartass one. Both Paul and Shawn had badgered him about that. They soon knew they wouldn't be doing that again.

"Uncle Steve," Paul said, with surprise and relief, as the rescue party emerged from the snowy fog.

"Anybody want a Snickers bar?" Shawn asked, attempting bravado with a wan smile but not able to control the tremulous tone of his voice.

Paul's voice cut into the icy mist. "Is Dad OK?"

Bouncing Back

"'Cause ya know what my momma always said, ..."

Lucille paused and lit up a cigarette, using the dashboard lighter, and nicked a long, hot-red-polished nail as she pushed the lighter back in.

"Damn. Broke another nail. Third one since we started this trip, and here we are . . . wherever we are . . . and Inez is all the way back there in Fincastle. I don't let no one other than Inez near these nails. Like my nails, Ralph? Candy Apple Supreme. Inez says it's all the rage over in Blacksburg. Well, I like it . . . a lot."

Lucille reached over and pulled the cigarette tray open. Ralph slapped at her hand with a "harumph" and hunkered himself over the steering wheel while Lucille rolled down her window a notch and tried to flick ashes to the winds. The force of the car's momentum drove them back inside, and Lucille patted the sparks dead on the flounces in her once-white blouse.

"Hells, bells, Ralph. Don't drive so fast. If you won't let an ash tray do the job God gave it, at least drive slow enough so's I can get the ashes outta the car."

Ralph sped up and squared himself more solidly behind the wheel, eyes firmly on the road, the veins in his neck standing out real strong.

"Anyway, as I was sayin', you know what my momma always . . . Ralph. Ralph, baby, wouldn't it have been a good idea to take that turn back there?"

The old Cadillac Seville just kept pointing straight down the road. Ralph's knuckles were white on the steering wheel.

"She always said, 'Lucille, you are just like a bouncing ball. No matter what happens, you just bounce right back. It's your gift, honey. Use it well.' That's what she always said, 'No matter what happens, you just bounce right back.' And it's just like my ex, Danny, said—my second ex, that is; Timmy was my first, as you well know . . . goodness gracious, Ralph,

21

you almost hit that little ole lady at her mail box. I don't know what's come over you of late. My momma always told me that you'd snap one of these days. But she said, 'Lucille, you don't need to worry none, because you're just like an ole bouncing ball. You just keep on bouncing up, no matter what.'"

Lucille lit up again, and, for the first time, Ralph turned his eyes from the road and stared daggers at her until she flicked the cigarette out of her slitted window. Ralph's eyes went back to front and center and Lucille popped in a couple of sticks of chewing gum. She scooted a foot out of a sling-back high heel. She proceeded to prop it up on the Seville's dash and started poking around the edges of the hot-red nails with the edge of an emery board. Lucille's gum snapped, and Ralph took in a extra-large lungful of air and slowly let it out.

"What I don't understand is why you don't just stop at a gas station and ask for some directions. You said you thought we'd find the interstate more than a half hour ago. But I don't see no interstate. Do you see an interstate, Ralph? Do you? Now there's a gas station right up ahead there. We could stop there and you could ask directions."

Lucille snapped her gum again, and Ralph's knuckles got even whiter on the steering wheel.

"Well, there's probably another gas station up the road a bit. I agree that that one looked a little seedy. Bet they didn't even have a usable ladies room." Down went one foot and up went the other. Snap went Lucille's gum.

"Hey, look, there's another gas station. Pull over, Ralph. I gotta go. You need gas anyway, and you could always ask for directions to the interstate from here."

The Seville slowed down and eased over beside a pump. Lucille gathered up a bag from the backseat, opened the passenger door, and stepped out.

"Just be a minute, hon. A girl's gotta make herself pretty for her man, ya know." Snap went Lucille's gum as she tap tapped around the side of the building on her sling-back high heels in short strides restricted by her tight skirt.

Twenty minutes later, a door at the side of the building opened, and Lucille came tap tapping back toward the gas pumps. Halfway to the pumps, though, she came to a stop and just gawked. No Seville at the pumps. She swiveled her blonde beehived head in both directions. No Seville in front of the station or over by the air hose. No Seville over in front of what looked like a mom and pop diner next to the gas station. Her eyes went back to the gas pumps, willing an old red Cadillac Seville to materialize there. But there still was no Seville parked at the pump. What was parked at the pump was a beat-up old blue Samsonite two-suiter suitcase. Lucille's suitcase; sitting up on its hinges right in the road beside the pump.

Lucille's eyes narrowed and she surveyed the landscape again. Two men were plastered at the grimy window over at the gas station office, staring at her real hard. But when she met their stares, they looked embarrassed and their faces disappeared from the window.

Lucille stood there for several minutes, waiting for reality to set in. But the reality that was setting in wasn't the one she was looking for. At length, she gave a sigh, sat down on the suitcase, and dug around in her purse for a cigarette and an emery board. She remembered what her mother always said, and she'd just sit here and wait for Ralph to return and give her a perfectly good explanation for this.

An hour later, the sun was getting pretty hot and Lucille was still sitting on her suitcase beside the gas pumps. She'd smoked her last two cigarettes and filed all three offending hot-red-polished nails nearly to the quick. She was just fishing around in her empty cigarette pack one more time, without any real hope of finding anything, really, when one of the station attendants, the younger and better-looking one, approached her with shuffling steps and his eyes plastered to the ground like he was avoiding stepping in a puddle of oil or something, and she just waved him away with a devil-may-care lilting laugh.

"He'll be back in a few minutes. My husband's just gone on an errand. Everything's fine, hon. Thanks. I'll just set here a spell. Say, you don't happen to have a cigarette for a lady, do ya?"

Still not looking directly at her, his face beet red, the attendant pointed to Lucille's empty cigarette pack with one hand and the nearby gas pump with the other and then made a mushroom-cloud gesture over his head with both hands.

"Sure, hon," Lucille responded with her best happy camper laugh. "I get the picture. How about a stick of gum then?"

The attendant searched around in his pockets and came up with a grimy, crinkled, yellow-papered stick of gum, which he handed over to Lucille with a blush and an apologetic look, and then he turned and scurried back to the safety of the station office. He didn't disappear far into the building, though. Lucille noted that both men had their faces plastered to the window again, and both looked embarrassed and concerned. She assumed their concern was for her, and she arched her back, crossed her legs, and pointed her toes primly for their benefit.

It was getting on toward dark, and Lucille and her suitcase were still taking up space beside the pump. Luckily, business hadn't been very good and nobody had needed Lucille's pump yet. Lucille was a little shaken now. She'd just gone through the litany of what her mother had always said about her, and one of her momma's frequent sayings had just popped up for the first time. It's what she'd said about Ralph. She'd said—more than once—that Ralph had that impatient, wandering streak in him and that someday, if Lucille didn't watch out, he was going to up and leave her. Lucille had always thought that her momma was saying something about a weakness Ralph had at those times, but now . . .

It was at this low point in Lucille's mood that the younger station attendant materialized again with a paper cup full of hot coffee and a shy, sympathetic smile.

"Thanks, hon," Lucille responded with a warm smile of her own. "Coffee's good, but a girl gets hungry now and then too. Don't suppose you know where I can get a bite to eat, do ya?"

The young man grinned big and pointed to the diner next door, the end of which looked like it was leaning a little to the left from Lucille's vantage point but which was now lit up like a Christmas tree and doing pretty good business, if the number of cars parked outside was any indication.

Lucille sighed and rose from her suitcase. The young man picked the case up and backed toward the station office, never taking his eyes from Lucille. Knowing she was being watched, Lucille gave a little extra swing to her hips as she tap tapped on her sling-back high heels and inside her tight skirt toward the diner. As she got closer, she saw the "Help Wanted" sign in the diner window, and her spirits bounced up. Just like her momma always said to her, . . .

Joleen Finds Her Voice

Gill was sitting on the porch, rocking and rubbing the head of that old hound dog of his, as Joleen walked up the stone path from the mailbox at the edge of the muddy road. She had walked slow uphill from the bus stop in the nearest town, at the mouth of a fold back into the Blue Ridge. The suitcase she was lugging, balanced on the other side by her guitar case, was heavy, but she wasn't walking slow because of that weight. She was weighed down by something more serious than that.

She worried that Gill would know it as soon as he saw her—that, like his momma, he could see guilt from miles away—or maybe that he could smell it on her. She'd be in for quite a licking if he did. And that would probably be the least of her worries.

Gill turned a wary eye on her as she approached. Buck, the hound dog, looked up, starting a woof as he did, but seeing that it was just his master's woman—and no threat to him in the pecking order around here—he yawned, lowered his muff to between his splayed legs again, and snorted off into sleep.

"Did'ja bring back enough to leave somethin' after paying for the trip and makin' up for your absence?" Gill asked when Joleen had reached the bottom step of the rickety porch. "You know I tol' you this nonsense would stop if it didn't more than pay for itself."

Joleen sighed, set the suitcase down on the dirt and gravel that passed for a lawn at the fringe of the porch steps, placed the guitar case on top of that, and climbed the steps. She crossed over Gill's foot without him moving it and sank into the other rocker, with a second sigh.

"Here. $500. Hope that's enough," she said as she scrounged around in her purse and came up with an envelope stuffed with fifty-dollar bills. "I done pretty good in Roanoke, honey. Won the talent contest and then . . ."

But she saw that Gill wasn't even listening to her. He had his eyes on the greenbacks as he closed his hand over the proffered money. The bills were still in Joleen's hand when he did that. Gill stood up from the rocker, still holding Joleen's hand in his grip. "Well, let's go into the house then. I want some."

"Oh, Gill," Joleen answered, trying to keep the tired whine out of her voice. "It's afternoon yet. And I've just walked the three miles from town—after the long bus ride from Roanoke—and there's some chores needin' done, I'm sure."

"You been gone five days, Joleen. What 'ja expect I'd want when you got back? Git on in the house now."

Buck raised his head and gave a little growl as Joleen walked past him into the house. Greenbacks didn't impress him much—nor did the woman's reappearance in his life.

From the minute they entered the house Joleen expected Gill to stop and hold and snarl his, "You been with another man, ain't you?" But it never came. Gill was concentrating hard on getting his own pleasure out of her.

He hadn't even asked her what she'd won the $500 for doing in the talent contest.

The man in Roanoke had been older and uglier than Gill, but at least he'd given her some time and attention.

It wasn't her first beauty pageant—she'd had to win a few to get this far—but it was sort of make-or-break time for her now. There hadn't been too many Miss Virginias older than she would be come November. The state pageant was held down in Roanoke, and it had been hell to pay to get Gill to let her go from out of their Blue Ridge, Virginia, hollow to compete. She was sure if the event had been held in Norfolk, he wouldn't have let her go, like he didn't let her go last year when it was up in Fairfax, in Northern Virginia. Roanoke was farther away then he'd ever let her travel before.

He was jealous that way, even though it usually seemed that he cared more for his hound dog than for her. But she'd shown him the list of prize money, and he'd begrudgingly told her she could try it, although he thought it looked like a lot of foolishness. When she'd asked him if he

27

was coming to cheer her on, he just gave her his "Are you from outer space?" look and asked her if she didn't realize how important his job was down at the service garage in town.

When Joleen had won the talent contest with her singing and guitar playing, she realized for the first time that she had a shot at the finals. The top woman went straight to the nationals with the Miss Virginia title, and the next two would get to go on to Nashville for a regional Miss South contest, with the winner of that also going to the national pageant.

She reasoned later that this had probably been her downfall that had led her into sin—the glimmer of a hope for getting further.

She'd been in the ballroom of the Hotel Roanoke convention center, waiting along with all of the other girls for the construction workers and designers to stop fussing on stage so that they could practice their evening gown walk, when she'd heard the page over the loudspeaker.

"Miss Worthington . . . Miss Nelson County, to the reception desk, please." That was her, Joleen. Both of them were her. She was a Worthington. Gill was a Scragg, but, thankfully, she was still a Worthington. But she also was Miss Nelson County. That was her title—the county she represented in the pageant.

When she went to hotel reception, the man behind the desk held out a folded note to her. "Please meet me in the Starbucks three blocks to the north now," was what was written, but what was important was that it was signed, "One who can make a difference."

As soon as she saw him sitting there, drinking his coffee inside the Starbucks, Joleen knew what this was about. It was the head judge of the pageant.

Perhaps if this wasn't probably her last-chance year— and more perhaps if she hadn't won the talent contest and wasn't standing at least on the lower step of the finals podium already—and perhaps if her life wasn't just too, too dreary to not try to break out of, Joleen wouldn't have gone to the man's car. But she did. When he pulled up beside a seedy motel, though, Joleen ran out of courage while he was, as he said, getting a "taste of her," and she managed to put him off the hunt—politely, she thought.

"No hard feelings?" she'd said, hoping he wasn't mad at her.

"Naw, honey. I just wanted to be with a winner. I'm sure you'll win."

What he'd said made Joleen feel real good. Only later did she feel the guilt, and her greatest sin was that she didn't feel the guilt until she had won the second runner-up spot. She was sure that he had promised her the crown.

When she had managed to maneuver him to where only he could hear her whisper and had voiced her pique, he merely smiled and murmured that he'd only said she'd win—not what she'd win—and if she had really wanted the crown, she should have given him what Miss Fairfax had.

Months later she would feel fortunate that she hadn't won the crown—that she'd gone to Nashville next rather than straight to Atlantic City.

When she'd gotten home from Roanoke, there was only one thing on Gill's mind. Even Buck didn't give her a woof; he just lifted his head, gave her a dismissive look, and rolled over for Gill to reach down and rub his belly before pushing Joleen into the house.

Joleen knew she was second best to Gill's hound. And that Buck didn't care any more than Gill did that she was now the second runner-up to Miss Virginia—or even that she'd come home with $500 for that matter.

Not for the first time she wondered how she'd feel if Gill asked her to marry him—not that the thought had ever entered his mind, she was sure. But if he did, she knew her world would crumble into nothingness. Whatever she did from this point in her life, she knew her life was going to have to get better. She'd see to that herself. She was the second runner-up to Miss Virginia.

* * * *

Only in Nashville could Joleen have had the revelation that came to her.

As soon as she arrived there for the Miss South pageant, she realized she was badly out of her depth. There was beauty on all sides of her in the dressing rooms. Perfect beauty. Manufactured beauty. Scraped-on beauty. Joleen's was a natural, interesting beauty. That no longer cut it in the realm of beauty pageants. What was interesting, intriguing, attracting in her features was a flaw in the eyes of the system at this level.

Reality assaulted her at every turn. She would have been crushed, would have wanted to open her veins and just melted away if . . . if she hadn't won the talent competition in Nashville just as she had in Roanoke.

This meant she could go home to Gill with prize money in hand—more than $1,000 this time. He wouldn't care where it had come from, what part of the competition had provided it. He took her beauty as just his right—his right as the biggest stud in Nelson County—his right to claim the county rose and to use her until she was wan and flaccid from too many pregnancies and calloused and worn out from a hardscrabble life. That she had a clear-toned mournful soprano voice that could loosen hearts and moisten tear ducts and was matched with a sure stroke of the guitar strings meant nothing to him. He didn't even realize it. As far as Joleen knew, Gill had never stayed around to hear her sing. All he knew or wanted of her was that, by his having her, no other man in Nelson County could.

Being in Nashville, home of country music, and winning the beauty pageant talent contest with her country music songs provided groundwork for the revelation. Billy Ray Furness provided the rest.

Billy Ray was the darling of the Miss South pageant. He was about the biggest talent producer in Nashville, and the pageant bowed and scraped to him because he was providing the nationally acclaimed country music legends of song as the glue that would hold the regionally televised final night ceremonies of the pageant together.

Where he walked in the halls of the events pavilion, people genuflected. Whatever he wanted, he got.

The evening of the final judging of talent, he got all starry-eyed at Joleen's performance. He made no bones about talking it up in the hearing of the judges and Joleen alike. He said she could be a recording star—that he could make her a star and that wouldn't it be wonderful publicity for the pageant to have the story of a star born on their stage floating around in the national entertainment media?

The selection of Joleen as the winner of that portion of the competition was universal, almost by acclaim. And the applause for her impromptu encore was even more thunderous than for her winning performance.

The pageant officials were delighted to provide Billy Ray a very private dressing room backstage when he told them he'd have a proposition to put to Joleen that would launch a major career. The pageant officials were giddy with joy not only on Joleen's behalf but also on behalf of their publicity department.

The proposition Billy Ray had to give to Joleen amid declarations of what a star she would be and how closely they could work together as country singer and mentor business manager only belatedly sank in with Joleen when he closed and locked the door of the very private dressing room. All Joleen could think of was how she had messed up and ended up as a second runner-up before and how Billy Ray was pointing to a career that had opened up to her by coming to Nashville rather than Atlantic City—built not on fleeting physical beauty but on her talent as a country singer.

The next morning, Joleen couldn't find Billy Ray anywhere, nor could anyone she talked to tell her how she could contact him. The closest she got to tracking him down was the vague suggestion that he had left that morning for Los Angeles.

Joleen might have returned to the hollow in the folds of the Blue Ridge in despair if it had not been for the revelation. She need not try to make the most of fleeting beauty. Her voice would far outlast that. She was a country singer. Billy Ray had had his little fun, but the applause in that

31

large auditorium was real. And it had made love to her in ways and to depths no man had.

When she arrived at the mailbox on the verge of the muddy road in a taxi, Gill just stood up from his rocker and waited for her to climb the front porch stairs. Buck gave her the usual woof of derision, and Gill closed his hand over the one Joleen proffered her contest win prize money in and led her into the farmhouse.

* * * *

Not surprisingly, Gill hadn't asked what Joleen had won to be bringing home a good chunk of money—or why she'd driven up in a taxi rather than walking home from the bus station—and, most interesting of all, why she said she had another beauty pageant to go to in Richmond that might last two weeks. She brought money home, and as long as she did that and followed him into the farmhouse in the shadow of the Blue Ridge when she came back, that was enough for Gill. He had enough to worry about down at the service garage. He didn't have time to check on whether or not there was a beauty pageant on in Richmond.

Gill was so taken with trying to figure out what was going amiss with the transmission on the mayor's Cadillac that he didn't even notice that when Joleen left for Richmond, she packed three bags, rather than the one—enough to hold all of her clothes and her momma's silver—and left in a taxi. Buck noticed, though. He stood on the porch and wagged his tail while Joleen hauled the bags and guitar case out to the taxi in two loads—right under Gill's nose. If it could be said a dog smiled, Buck was smiling.

Joleen always did say that Buck had more brains than Gill did.

She had made all of the arrangements in Richmond beforehand. A recording studio and an experienced sound technician, a nice young guy named Paul. Joleen thought he had a great smile. And he was ultrapolite, yes ma'ming her left and right and being real attentive to all of her requests as she sat there, in the recording booth, for hours, and sang her haunting laments, all her own creations—all the flowing forth of short, but hard, years of trials and tribulations.

After they were done, Joleen just sat there, exhausted, in the silence. No applause, no nothing. She stood up from the stool and walked into the sound booth. Paul was sitting there, looking down at his controls.

"Well?" she asked, not sure she wanted to hear his reaction.

He looked up, and quietly said, "Wow. Just wow."

Joleen wondered what he meant, though. He was looking vaguely at the level of her tits. But if he thought he was going to get anything, he was sadly mistaken. She'd paid him in cash for his time. She was a little irritated. Is that what they all are thinking of, she wondered. He had seemed to be a nice guy.

"What are you going to do with this recording?" he asked.

"Start trying to sell it around, I guess," she answered. She knew it wasn't going to be easy, though. She knew after a couple of weeks she'd have to find some work. She sure as hell knew she wasn't going back to Nelson County and Gill.

"OK if I see if I can get them someplace?" he asked.

"Sure, why not?" she answered.

A week later, Paul called her at her motel and said he might have a proposition for her. Could she meet him at the West End Starbucks on Broad? It was near her motel; she knew he knew it was near her motel.

Here we go again, she thought. But nothing had panned out in Richmond yet. She'd found Billy Ray's address in Nashville and sent the recording off there—as well to other music producers in Nashville—but she'd heard nothing back.

So, OK, if this Paul has a better lead than she had developed so far, yes, she'd give him what he wanted. But he'd better have more than just empty promises. She'd been too far down that road already. It was time for her to be the one using and taking advantage of someone else.

Paul was looking real good when she showed up at Starbucks. He was nattily dressed—all groomed, like he wanted them to video the results of his proposition. If he got lucky.

"You're late," he said. He looked almost panicked about that. "I was afraid you wouldn't come."

"I almost didn't," Joleen said. "I've been around this proposition in Starbucks deal once too often."

"Shush," he said.

"Shush what? Why?" Joleen answered, a little piqued.

"Just shush and listen. Sit down and listen. Listen to the music."

Joleen sat. And Joleen began to listen. And Joleen realized she was listening to Joleen—coming from the radio. One of her own songs, sung by her. And then, after that ended, she heard another of her songs, again sung by her. Coming over the speakers on the radio.

She was trembling, her palm on top of Paul's on the table top. She felt him tremble too, enjoying the experience as much as she was—and not just the experience of hearing herself on the radio.

"You got my songs on the radio here in Richmond?" she asked.

"Yeah. I've got a few connections. They ate them right up. And not just here in Richmond. This is a syndicated show. This is going out all over the South."

Joleen's cell phone was buzzing. A text message. Billy Ray Furness. "Where did u go? We were going to talk contract. Call me," it said. Joleen flipped the phone off. She'd see what he had to offer later, but he wasn't high on her list at the moment.

Paul had done this for her. No strings attached. He'd just gone ahead and done it. Hadn't demanded or asked anything from her.

"That was a Nashville record producer," she said. "Already talking recording contract."

"That's good. But go slow. There will be others."

"You'll help me?"

"If you want. Any way you want."

34

They paused, frozen in place, Joleen's hand on Paul's again. They were both looking at the hands, as if they probably should let loose, but neither wanted to.

"Should we celebrate? Go someplace and celebrate?" Joleen murmured.

"If you like," Paul said.

"My motel room OK?" Joleen asked. She was already thinking ahead. She knew he'd be good and attentive.

"Maybe we should go slow on that," Paul said.

"You don't want—?"

"Sure I do. Of course I do. But you should be sure and shouldn't, you know, have it be because of any of this. You have more hours at the studio. We could go to the studio. Do you have any more songs in you?"

"You bet, I do." And then she smiled. "And I see some happier songs boiling up inside me too."

Back on the porch of the Nelson County farmhouse, Gill was sitting and rocking, thinking somewhere in the back of his mind, somewhere in back of reviewing the brake relining job he had to do in the morning, that it should be about time for Joleen to be coming come from that fool pageant in Richmond. She'd better have some good cash in hand, was all he thought.

He stirred, hearing the sound of the radio cutting through his other thoughts. Some woman was singing a sad song on the radio. The voice sounded sort of familiar and the song was real pretty. But he couldn't quite place who was doing the singing.

At his side, flattened out on the worn wood of the porch, Buck, recognizing the voice instantly, put his paws over his ears and emitted a low moan.

35

The Invisibles

She hadn't even wanted the bracelet. She'd just never had anything that nice before, even though it wasn't her style. Not that she had a style. She deserved something and didn't think anyone would notice that she took it, because she was used to being overlooked, to just not being seen. And if no one noticed, who was there to care? There were a lot of other bracelets hanging there; one shouldn't have been missed. It would have been nice if Shayla hadn't seen her lift that bracelet, though. Shayla was supposed to be a friend of hers. Shayla took her summer job entirely too seriously, Cindy Sue thought. Not something you should go out of your way to call out a friend on. Shayla could have just looked the other way. Those stores made allowances for losing things. And how much could a bracelet from a Dollar Store be worth anyway?

It had been her birthday. The day after her birthday, actually. Neither her mother nor that good-for-nothing boyfriend of her mother's had so much as wished her a good day. Jake had made a pass at her, but there wasn't anything unusual in that—or personal, she didn't allow. Jake would spike any female who would have him. Cindy Sue didn't know why her mother kept him around. It's not like he brought any money into the house. But then he was a lot younger than her mother and good-looking too. Thought a lot of himself, he did. Of course, quite a few of the girls thought a lot of him too. She bet they all thought she was letting Jake mess with her. It was the only time she got any attention from them, though—them wanting to know about him and what he did with a girl.

Cindy Sue stopped, out of breath from the climb. She looked around. She'd been following Mine Branch up into the Blue Ridge from Crimora, but now that she looked around, she realized the stream had petered out. She wondered how long she'd been following a disappearing trickle of water. She sat down on a rock and pulled the knapsack off her back.

She'd run right out of the Dollar Store, with Shayla hollering bloody murder at her back, and went straight home and threw her cell phone, some panties, a pair of shorts, and a couple of T-shirts, and enough food for a string of days in her backpack. Then she'd hauled on out of there. Her mother was at work. And, thank god, Jake wasn't anywhere around. She didn't have time to fight him off with a broom before she had to be on her way.

She guessed they'd figure she'd head south to become lost in Waynesboro, so she headed for the mountains. That was a laugh, though. She could stand, naked in the center of Crimora and no one in town would see her.

She hadn't even come away with the bracelet. She'd let that drop on the sidewalk outside the store entrance. She'd figured anyone following her would stop to pick it up and would give her enough of a head start.

Her birthday and she couldn't even give herself a present.

It had taken her three days to get this far, nearly to the top of the ridge of the Blue Ridge mountains. She was tired and her feet were screaming at her. She hadn't talked to another solitary soul in that whole time. It was just like she didn't exist.

She checked the bars in the cell phone. They were strong enough for a call. Once she was over the top of the ridge she didn't know if she could get reception. She punched in Brenda's number. Brenda was maybe her only friend, and that seemed only to hold when it suited Brenda and there were no better prospects around.

"Brenda, it's me."

"Me who?"

"Cindy Sue."

"Hi, there, Cissy. Haven't heard from you in a couple of days. Been hanging out with that boyfriend of your mother's?"

Brenda didn't sound surprised or excited or anything. "I'm on a trip. Anybody been asking for me?"

"Not that I've heard. Did you hear about Rachel. She's carrying, and she says it's Pete Winter's. Can you imagine that?"

"No, do tell. The bus looks like it's ready to pull out, so I gotta go. Just was checking in."

"Bus?"

Cindy Sue didn't respond. She'd already clicked off. Nobody had missed her. Maybe after Shayla had calmed down, she hadn't said anything to anybody about the bracelet after all. Cindy Sue was still on this side of the ridge. She could just turn around and go home. To what, though?

She looked around. It was peaceful up here. And so green and quiet. Really beautiful. She decided she'd rest right here and climb that last little bit tomorrow.

By noon of the next day, she was at the summit. She knew that because she was standing next to the Skyline Drive and the terrain dipped down the mountainside both east and west of that. She retreated back below a rock wall when she heard a car coming down the drive and then, when it had passed, she dashed across the road and started downhill. Charlottesville. She'd go down into Charlottesville, get a job, and be someone people noticed. Maybe she'd dye her hair pink and get a nose ring.

The middle of the next day she sensed she knew where she was. Before he'd disappeared, her dad had brought the kids to the Sugar Hollow Reservoir a couple of times and then on upstream from there to a multichambered swimming hole carved out of the rocks. Her dad had been fun—when he was around. He'd noticed her. He looked directly at her, not through her, and he'd actually ask her questions. He just hadn't stayed around for the answers.

She floated in the water of the swimming hole. She hadn't bathed for what, nearly a week now? How long had she been gone? Was it five days now or six?

And no one had come looking for her.

It was nice, real nice here at the swimming hole. She could just live here forever. Get herself a nice little cabin and just live away from the world in these beautiful mountains. Bet nobody would find her.

She heard voices coming up the trail and scampered out of the water, grabbed her clothes, and melted into the trees.

The voices were a jolt. Other than the phone call with Brenda, she hadn't talked to anyone for nearly a week now.

She wanted to talk with someone—to connect—but not with any strings or fuss. She wasn't far from the summit, so after pulling her clothes on, she climbed back up there. When she got to the top, she could have kicked herself for not checking her bars before making the effort. But the cell phone was still good. She called Brenda again.

"You didn't tell me you'd run off, Cissy," Brenda said. Her voice was breathless and sounded excited now, as if she was at the center of something. "Where are you? There are posters out on you. Your mother's boyfriend has been pulled in and they're talking to him about where you might be."

"So, my mother is looking for me?"

"Not that I've heard. It was your grandmother. You were supposed to up and babysit for her in Grottoes or something. They're saying your mother didn't even know you were missing. Or so she claimed."

"Have you told anybody you talked with me?"

"No. I didn't know if you'd want me to. But they're questioning your mother's boyfriend."

"Good. Don't tell anybody we've talked yet, OK? I don't know if I want to come back."

She knew she shouldn't have left it like that. But if her mother hadn't even known she was gone . . . and if her grandmother's main concern was being out of a babysitter. . . . Maybe she'd just let them stew a bit. Maybe she'd just be invisible for a while longer.

She started back down the eastern slope of the Blue Ridge. A couple of more days and she was down, past the reservoir, and on flat ground again. She also was out of food and was hungry.

She walked to an intersection that claimed it was the town of White Hall, but there wasn't much more than a general store and a few houses and a narrow road dumping into a wider road. It didn't even cross it. A general store was what she wanted, though. It wasn't a bracelet she needed to lift anymore. Now it was food and maybe a six-pack of Coke. She was hungry—and not just for attention or thinking she deserved a birthday present, even if she had to steal it herself because no one else remembered it had been her birthday.

She entered the store and started walking the aisles. There was a young guy—pretty good looking—at the cash register. He was watching her every move, so she guessed this wasn't going to be an easy proposition.

The word "Crimora" hit her face from a copy of the Waynesboro newspaper that was on a stand just inside the store entrance. She went over and looked at it. The face of Brenda stared back at her. It had been an auto accident. Drinking had been involved. Brenda hadn't been driving, but she was the one who was dead. The only person Cindy Sue had talked to since she herself had disappeared, and now she was dead. Cindy Sue wondered if Brenda had had the time or inclination to say anything before the accident about her having called. But she thought not. Brenda had always liked to have secrets. Cindy Sue thought she should work up some tears for Brenda's passing, but she was just too weary and hungry at this moment. Maybe later. Brenda would just have to wait. She always made Cindy Sue wait to see if they were still friends on any given week.

* * * *

Zeb woke up to the silence. He listened for his mother's steady breathing from the other room, but then he remembered. He'd buried his mother three weeks earlier. He was all alone now in Bobcat Hollow. Not another soul in here now. This is the way his people wanted it, but Zeb didn't think that any of them had ever thought the family would get down to just one. And even if so, they'd likely not to have been pleased to learn it was him.

He lived in a two-over-two house that had been here since before the war of northern aggression. It was stuck deep in the hollow in the shadow of the Blue Ridge, where nothing but a trail that you had to know was there to see it led. Zeb had to walk three miles just to get to where he stashed his old Ford 150 pickup. You could be flying right over the house in a helicopter and not know it was there.

That's what Zeb's folks, the Walkers, had counted on for nearly ninety years now. It was back in the late 1920s when some folks up in Washington decided that the Blue Ridge down to Rockfish Gap needed to be a national park. They didn't ask any of the folks who had settled and lived in those mountains for nearly three centuries what they thought of that idea, though. Ten years after deciding that, they decided that the mountain folk all had to go. For the next decade, they bought folks out, and those who wouldn't go were pushed and pulled out, so that by 1940 they declared that there were fewer than a hundred folks still living in the mountains and that they were so hard to catch up with that they could just die out.

What the people in Washington didn't know, though, was that it was going to take a lot longer than that for the people of the hollows to give up their way of life.

Zeb's folks, down from his grandparents, had just ignored the outside world and stuck back up in Bobcat Hollow in a fold between Pinestand and Cedar mountains. Zeb's granddaddy had made do with a plot of farmland they owned and worked in the valley west of Pasture Fence Mountain. And his daddy had ventured down into the White Hall area to help with the harvests. The Walker women, though, back as far as anyone had talked about, had stayed right here in the hollow, from the day they were born to the day they died.

There had been three families sticking out the evictions in the hollow, and doing so because the government agents didn't even know where this hollow was. They had married among themselves. And then there was only one. And now Zeb was all alone.

He'd worked a couple of years down in White Hall, at the general store there, and would continue to do so. But his heart was right here in Bobcat Hollow.

It was sort of lonely, though, without even his mother to come home to. And now there was so much to do to keep

41

the homestead going. He did miss his mother. He wasn't fond of a lot of yakking, but it was nice to have someone to talk to in the evenings. His mother had been good that way; she never was a yakker, but when she did say something, it had meaning.

Working in the White Hall general store wasn't too bad. Not too many folks came in, and most of those who did looked right through him—like he was invisible. They did their business and were gone.

He'd heard that some years before he'd come to work here there had been a group of old men who sat out on the store's front porch and jawed and chawed and rocked the day away. But they were all gone. And none of the younger men had replaced them. They all were going east, into Charlottesville, or south, to Crozet, to work—even if they came back to White Hall to live. But not many were staying here.

And no one asked him where he lived. No one asked him much of anything other than the price of something that had been missed in the labeling.

He liked it that way. Still he missed his mother. And someone to share the chores with up in Bobcat Hollow.

This morning he hadn't allowed time for firing up the cook stove. It would take him time to remember that he had to get up earlier if he wanted a hot breakfast on weekdays. He grabbed a couple of chunks of bread from the breadbox, pulled the jug of milk up from the cool stream running through the basement of the house, and poured himself a glass. And then he was off, down slope on the narrow trail to where he kept the pickup.

When he got to the store, he opened up and brought in the papers—the *Daily Progress* from Charlottesville and *Waynesboro News Virginian*—and brought them inside and placed them on the stand inside the door. He clucked his tongue at the sad news on the front of the Waynesboro paper about the young girl killed in the automobile accident over in Crimora. Liquor. That's why his parents and their parents had stuck to the hills, his mother always told him. Because young people were too anxious about killing themselves over something they had no business being into.

He noticed that a flyer had dropped out of one of the Waynesboro papers and he stooped down and picked it up.

Another troubled girl. A nice-looking girl, another one from Crimora, missing. He'd read about that in the Waynesboro paper the previous day. Obviously the mother's boyfriend was suspected. She was a good-looking girl in the photo on the flyer, but she looked sad. If he was going to put another word to it, he'd say she looked lonely. He felt sorry for her. Lost and probably never would be found. Invisible, just like him.

He went behind the counter and moved the vase of flowers more to the right, away from where folks would put their purchases down on the counter when he rang them up. That Mrs. Stevens, who worked the evenings. She had to have something to cheer the place up. She'd bring in flowers every day. These were yellow roses—probably from her own garden. They'd still be there in the morning, and Zeb always had to move them to the side.

As he was doing this, he heard the door open and a young woman walked in. He recognized her immediately. He'd just seen her in the missing person's brochure and the face, which had haunted him a bit with the aspect of the same loneliness he was feeling, had stuck with him. Cindy Sue something was her name.

He watched her move around the store. And he watched her giving him furtive glances. He wondered if she found him attractive. He thought he could find her attractive. If she'd just give some hint of a smile. She looked scared, though, and hungry. It dawned on him that she wasn't there to shop, really—that she, in fact, was hungry and didn't have the money to buy anything. He couldn't remember how long she'd been missing, but he thought maybe it had been a week or more. Had she had anything to eat in that time? How had she gotten over the mountain? Had she hitchhiked? White Hall wasn't really on any driven route over the mountains. Had she maybe walked over the mountain? All alone the whole time?

She went over to the newspaper stand, and he could see she was looking at the story on the girl who died in the auto wreck. Another girl from Crimora. He wondered if this Cindy Sue had known the other girl. Crimora wasn't much more of a town than White Hall was. They probably had known each other. He couldn't tell if she was working toward tearing up or something.

He had the sudden wish that she would open the paper and see the missing person poster—to see that someone missed her and was trying to find her. That she wasn't invisible like Zeb thought about himself. But then, with a glimmer of thought and wondering if Cindy Sue would like the house in Bobcat Hollow, he hoped she wouldn't open the paper.

To keep her from doing that, he cleared this throat, pulled a rose out of the vase, and spoke up. "Miss, you look like you could use a yellow rose. I think this would look pretty in your hair."

Cindy Sue looked up, surprised. But she also was pleased, and she gave Zeb a tentative smile.

"You look like you might be hungry too. Why don't you just pick out something you'd like to eat? And we have soft drinks in the cooler over there. No charge. We'll pretend it's your birthday or something."

"It . . . it *was* my birthday just the other day, as a matter of fact," Cindy Sue answered. And her smile broadened.

Converging Divergence

(Inspired by a combination of Louise Lawler's painting "How Many Pictures," viewable at http://www.skarstedt.com/exhibitions/2005-11-02_contemporary-art/#/images/1/, and other exhibits running at the University of Virginia art museum at the time, including drawings of the renovation of the pavilions on the University of Virginia lawn and art featuring Edgar Allan Poe.)

Escape. Beam me up. Yes, just take me, Ed was thinking as he stared into the photograph, wanting to move away from its tantalizing disappointment. Agitated, drawn, and repelled by the image that beckoned to him but wasn't accepting him. Numb, imprisoned. His jailer just standing there, jabbering with that . . . that witch. That evil demon. Taunting rejection. Yes, that was it. Inviting Ed to rise on its rays into the outstretched arms of heaven. Yet mocking him, leaving him numb. A prisoner.

This changed everything. All of his careful planning. Freeing himself and escaping her . . . Linda . . . at last. And her accursed black cat. Sitting there, hunched down and looking up at him . . . always. Staring at him with its one good eye. Condemning him. Knowing and just waiting to thwart his plans. The black cat had to go too. Why did they have to renovate Pavilion X? But maybe a good thing. If they'd found her there, behind the wall . . . before he'd beamed up, it would have all been for naught. And where had the cat gone? Must know where the black cat is before putting in that last brick. Tossing and turning in the night, hearing the crying. The muffled crying from behind the wall—the damning condemnation.

He had seen it clearly in the designs on the wall. The crevice in the basement of Pavilion X—the space behind the wall. Could Linda see it too? And that witch, that evil demon? Of course they saw it. They were on to him. They were both smiling at him, indulgently, knowingly—knowing that his bonds would hold. Assuming he was someplace far, far away—that he didn't know they were slowly stripping him of every ounce of dignity and freedom. Sucking the life right out of him. They had plans too. He knew it. Any minute now he'd be entombed in that steel box and descend to hell. Hell is what it was. Beamed down rather than up, like in the taunting photograph. Linda with her poking and prodding and false smiles. Holding him prisoner, watching him go mad, wanting him to go mad.

Another plan. Need another plan. Fire. Ed knew he could do that. Late at night, with only the luminescent eye of the fiendish black cat judging and condemning him. Everyone abed. A simple match and the gauzy curtains at the window of his prison. He could drag himself that far. The fall of the House of Ed. The blaze caught in reflection in the frightened eye of the black cat. Freedom. Not the perfect freedom, of course. But a good, cleansing, purifying freedom. And worth it, worth the expression on the cat's face when it realized the roar of the fire would drown out its accusing cries. Linda, the witch, and the black cat as much prisoners to fate as Ed then. Yes, that would be worth the sacrifice.

But the beams into the arms of heaven. Still taunting him with a rise that never came. The horrific photograph. Playing with his desire; mocking him. No more real power left to him to rise on his own. Would no one release him? This torture Linda was imposing on him. Facing him with the futility of it all. He would go mad bound before this onslaught of the reality of his nonexistence.

* * * *

"Dad, does this photograph speak to you?" Linda had broken from her conversation with Angela and looked down to see that Ed's arms were twitching and he was working his jaw, trying to overcome the stroke-imposed failure to form words and create sound.

"Oh, look, he's crying. There are teardrops on his cheek."

46

"Probably just muscle cramps, a reflexive response," Angela muttered. "I wouldn't put too much hope into it. I know you wanted to stimulate him with this art gallery visit, but . . ."

She let the sentence drift off. Ever the hopeful one. Linda just wouldn't face the facts with her father—that he was lost to her now.

"Do you like this one particularly, Dad?" Linda asked as she knelt down beside the wheelchair. Ed leaned away from her as much as he could and worked his jaw in a lost cause.

"It's called 'How Many Pictures.' How many pictures do you see, Dad? I don't see any. Looks like sunbeams to me. Does it make you happy, Dad? Do you find it uplifting?"

Linda looked up at Angela. "I think he likes this one. His arms are trembling." She sighed and stood back up. She patted Ed on the shoulder and readjusted his sweater.

"Look," she said through her own tears and a smile, "his eyes are gleaming. That's the old devilish look I once knew so well."

"I don't know why you do this to yourself, Linda," Angela said, pursing her lips. "I don't know why you try to keep him at home with you. It's made you a prisoner; it's consuming and destroying your life. He's not there; he doesn't care."

"If I can just make him content—in familiar surroundings—that's enough."

Angela snapped her jaw shut. They had been over this countless times before. It wasn't her place anymore to take it further. She and Ed had been divorced for nearly twenty years. She could see it was useless to reason with her daughter here and now. She knew that gleam in Ed's eye too. She and her daughter had always had different interpretations of that. It was like a deceptive photograph, the three of them looking at the same image, but each seeing something different.

"If I can tear you away from this photograph, I guess we should go home," Linda said. "We've been through all the exhibits—the Poe, the University architectural drawings, and this abstract photography exhibit."

The gleam in Ed's eye turned to fire as his jailer wheeled him toward the steel box that would drag him down to hell.

The Passing of Little Eddie

(Inspired by Kenneth Hayes Miller's "City Street," viewable at
http://www.virginia.edu/artmuseum/collections_NEW/the
_collections/American/Miller_Kenneth_Hayes.php)

The joy of the woman in the next bed, who had said she worked for the Catholic church, had been so infectious that Maria had completely forgotten her anxieties and doubts and had begun to hope. Only after Maria had left the University of Virginia hospital did the real world begin to unravel her life again. How ironic that only one of them would leave that hospital room with her expectations fulfilled. But it had been a joyful three days for Maria, at least. That was what she tried to remember.

Big Eddie hadn't known anything about it until after he'd gotten out of the Greensville Correctional Facility. It hadn't been hard for Maria to keep him from knowing; she'd always been sitting on the other side of a screen before he entered the visitation room, and he couldn't tell anything with her sitting down. She didn't know why she didn't tell him those three times she'd been able to visit Greensville in those eight months, but the time had never seemed to be right. Just for some reason she didn't think it would go down too good.

And, boy, did it not go down too good. When she'd brought him home to a small apartment in Charlottesville after his release, Big Eddie had denied that it had anything to do with him. And he'd slapped her hard before he calmed down. The first time he'd done that in almost a year—before they'd taken him off for trial.

"Get rid of it," he said when he calmed down.

"Get rid of it?" Maria mumbled through her tears and the hand covering her bruised cheek. "How?"

She wasn't brave enough to ask "why"—but that was the question thundering through her mind. She wasn't asking him to give it any time or effort. She'd worked all of that out, even with keeping her job.

"Toss it in the Rivanna," he said. "If not, I'll take care of it. I'm going out; if it's here when I get back, I'll take care of it myself."

Surely he wasn't serious—especially the part about the river—Maria thought. But when she'd looked in his eyes, she knew he was serious.

And that was that.

When he was gone, Maria sat in a kitchen chair, listening and thinking. If a summoning cry came at this moment, she would melt. But all was quiet. She had dreamed of it being quiet like this, but now that this would be her future, her heart was breaking.

She sighed, rose from the chair, and moved around the apartment like a zombie, dressing in her best suit—the blue one she saved for special days at the office. She pulled her red church hat down from the top shelf of the closet and dug the black stole she knitted herself out of the drawer and draped it on the back of the kitchen chair. Such an event as this required her to look her best. There was so much sin to cover up. She had to look her Sunday best.

Returning to the open drawer, she stared down at it for a moment. A tear fell on a small blue blanket. With another sigh, she reached in and pulled everything out of the drawer and trudged backed to the kitchen. She placed the contents of the drawer in the bottom of a milk crate and smoothed out the top blanket with a faltering, caressing touch.

Next she walked over to her bed and returned with a bundle and placed the treasure on the padding of clothes in the milk crate.

She took a bus down to the center of Charlottesville. She got off at Market Street at the central library to walk up to Jackson Park. She walked up to East Jefferson and turned toward the east. Now that she was here, she wasn't sure how far away the river was. Neither her parents, from a farm up near Stanardsville, nor Big Eddie had ever let her come down to old town Charlottesville.

"Our kind don't mix with that kind," her daddy had said. "They're rich snobs. A lot of folks from somewhere else. Don't have roots here like we do."

Well, Maria didn't suppose that those she'd grown up with on farms in the shadow of the Blue Ridge were any more real Virginians than those in Charlottesville were. She'd been scared to look up who came first because she was afraid it wasn't her daddy's ancestors and she'd mouth off about it someday and be fisted over the moon. Both her Pa and Big Eddie were good for that.

The Holy Comforter Church on East Jefferson, one block up from Market. That's where the woman had said she worked. And she'd said it wasn't far from there to the Rivanna.

Maria had had to ask, but the first person she asked knew exactly where she wanted to go. It was just down the block from where she was standing when she asked for directions.

She walked around the block the church was on three times. She told herself she was waiting for dusk and she didn't want anyone to see her at that important moment. But the truth was that she didn't want that moment to come at all. There would be no turning back then. Her life would never be the same again.

She knew it had to be near five o'clock when the moment came.

It was almost time now. It was now—her way. If she couldn't do it, it would be Big Eddie's way. She put the crate down at the head of an alley, fumbled around in her purse, and took out a scrap of paper and a pin. She took one last look at what she had worked so hard over in writing on the paper. In the end, it had been just four words.

"His name is Edmund," it said. She wanted to write "Edmund, Junior," but she was afraid that would find its way back to Big Eddie. She leaned down and pinned the note to the blanket covering her sleeping baby boy, picked the crate up, and trudged east toward the direction she'd been told the river was.

51

She stood across the street, up toward Jackson Square, staring at the steps of the Holy Comforter Church, willing the woman to walk out of the church and down the stairs.

Her prayers were answered.

The church woman, who had so much wanted a baby, and whose baby had died in the hospital before Maria left with her newborn Little Eddie, found the baby and picked him up from the milk crate.

Maria took one last, lingering look as passersby gathered around the woman on the church steps and the precious bundle, and then she turned and started walking with heavy steps back toward the Market Street bus stop.

Thanks Rosa

I probably should have gotten a clue from Rudi's face when I got on the bus. But I didn't. I was too down in the "humphs" and trying not to feel guilty about cutting the dental care meeting at city hall. But I'd had it up to the gills with all of these dead-end meetings. All I wanted to do now was get back to my apartment, turn off the lights, and pout in my old, comfortable La-Z-Boy recliner.

It was the smile. Rudi was smiling. Rudi never smiled. I'd been riding his bus home from the Downtown Mall for three years and Rudi had never smiled at me.

"Afternoon, Dave. Turned out nice, didn't it?"

Shock. I'd introduced myself many times before, a congenital habit of a community planning advocate, but I'd had no idea my name had sunk in with Rudi.

I smiled wanly, muttered something resembling "Yes, indeed, nice day," and turned to clump down the aisle. That was the best I could do. Rudi had picked a bad day to turn human. I wasn't human myself at the moment. My low-income housing program wasn't going well—not well at all. I wanted to feel sorry for myself. It all seemed a wasted effort.

"Afternoon, young man. Beautiful day."

She was sitting there, primly, on the front seat of the bus, or rather her bulk was spread out across the seat. But that didn't stop her from embodying the perfect southern lady: starched dress, strawlike hat with a rather tired rose, white gloves, broad smile. A perfectly proper black southern lady off to Sunday church. But this was Thursday, and my week was already set on interminable.

And I didn't know her from Mahalia Jackson, who she closely resembled. Another quick smile and another murmured agreement on yet another weather forecaster miscall and I was headed for the back of the bus.

As I struggled against the force of the now-moving bus, I instinctively looked down at my feet. This must be one of those dragging-toilet-paper-behind-me days, I thought.

They were sorry for me and making fun of me at the same time.

I folded myself into a cramped seat half way back in the bus and felt around for whatever was hanging or unzipped. I soon noticed, however, that it wasn't just me. Each time someone got on the bus, I saw Rudi nod and smile, and I heard the soft, mellow voice of the woman in the front seat giving a greeting.

I tried to bury my thoughts in the problems of my work. Three fruitless years trying to get things done in this town for its poor and disadvantaged and marginalized citizens. Time and effort wasted. Try as I might, though, whatever was going on at the front of the bus was blocking my funk.

The black woman got off on Preston Avenue, in front of the Zion Union Baptist Church, one stop before me, huffing and puffing as she leveraged herself off the seat and out the door after thanking a smiling Rudi profusely for the ride she'd paid for.

When my stop came up, I was determined to say something to Rudi, to ask him what all of this peculiar "niceness" was about—a personal affront on a day that I was determined to be grumpy and sorry for myself. He was welcoming someone else, so, while I waited, I turned and looked toward the back of the bus.

But the explanation wasn't in the back of the bus; it was in the front. Following Rudi's smile and gesture, I looked down at the now-empty seat the black madonna had been splayed across, and for the first time I saw the newly attached little metal plaque stitched to the center of that first seat on the bus.

The plaque read: "In honor of the memory of Rosa Parks."

I couldn't wait then for my turn to talk with Rudi. I flashed him a genuine smile and a "Thank you for the ride, Rudi" and hopped off the bus as quickly as I could. Suddenly reenergized, I hurried over to the bus shelter and hungrily examined the schedule on the wall, wondering how soon I could get turned around and back into the town center. I had an important meeting on dental care for the poor to get to at city hall.

The Photograph

Payne

Why had he left the photograph there on the dresser top? I had gone into his room to put his things together so they could take them down to Roanoke along with the body, and there it was. Almost like it was on exhibit, a challenging presence.

To a great extent Saddleback Creek Ranch's success had hinged on T. Jonas Duncan's patronage. Where T. Jonas Duncan went, everyone followed. He was the pied piper of celebrities, an icon of unique proportions.

A writer and nature photographer of legendary status, Duncan regularly came to our horse ranch south of Fincastle in the Shenandoah Valley in search of a horseback ride across the roof of the Blue Ridge Mountains and four-season photographs of the flora and fauna to be found there. At other times he could be found in the high Rockies, hunting elk, or in Canada or Alaska in search of more dangerous adventures.

Against that, coming to our part of the world seemed tame, and I'd always wondered why he kept coming back. I don't wonder about that anymore, though.

He wrote celebrated men's novels of male bonding in challenging and dangerous circumstances, themes, and situations that bring out the grit and nobility of strong and bold men. His writing inspired noble and strong and bold movies that won international awards on their own merits despite missing casting the ideal protagonist—T. Jonas Duncan himself, the epitome of the rugged, handsome, square-jawed, determined überman battling the elements, whatever they were—and winning and possessing largely and as he pleased.

He came to our ranch three or four times a year from the time I was a child, and my father took him up to the two horse trails at the top of the mountains Roanoke, to the east, was nestled in for as many days as it took to satisfy his yankering for riding and photographing. We all held him in awe. He had a rich, deep, expressive voice befitting his stature, both physical and intellectual, and he could tell a story as overpoweringly as he could write one. For years I would sit in the shadows just beyond the dining room as he dominated and enriched the dinner conversation.

I was at college, over at Virginia Tech in Blacksburg, when my dad died unexpectedly. We had our problems and had left much unsaid, but I loved him deeply. When he died, I had to quit college and take over the ranch. We could have gone under before I learned what I needed to know about dude ranching. But the first summer after my father's death Duncan came to the ranch as usual, and he made sure that the regular celebrities came back as well—and that new ones started to come. He saved us—me.

On one visit he spoke wistfully at dinner of missing his trips up into the Blue Ridge with my father. I, of course, offered to take him up on the horse trails as my father had done for over a decade. We owed him everything.

I had little idea how to be the cook, guide, and everything else for the three-day rides at the top of the Blue Ridge that had been my father's specialty, but Duncan was a patient man, a very patient man. By the end of the second day of riding, having started at the south end of the trail at the Peaks of Otter, being transported over the Roanoke River between trails by our ranch hand, Henry, to the northern trail, our horses were worn out.

"I do believe there's good sheltering just down the slope there a piece," Duncan said, as we let the horses drop their noses into the foam of a fast-moving stream.

"You think so?" I asked. "I think another mile on this loop on Chestnut Ridge is the Roanoke Mountain Camp Grounds, where we're supposed to camp."

"I think the place I remember is better—more private. It's where your father made camp when we came up here."

I followed his lead, leaving the trail and moving down the ridge between the enveloping trees. It didn't look all that promising to me. But then, when we'd ridden down the seam in the mountain bottomed by the stream, Duncan proved to be right.

"There's a stand of pine trees over there next to a stream," he said. "I think your dad and I have found good shelter in that ravine before."

We ate that night over an open fire, leaning against the saddles we had slung on the ground between the bank of the stream and the line of pines. Duncan was his charming best, weaving stores of male bonding and the raw challenge of man against nature in that rich baritone voice of his, in words that were strong and raw but also mesmerizing in their poetry.

The air was crisp and slightly chilly, and Duncan called me over to sit beside him as he leaned against his saddle so that we could share the blanket. He said we would be so much more comfortable making maximum use of our shared body heat. And I believed him. I had always believed him.

He talked to me about my father, and I started to cry, the grieving and the suspicions about my father's unexpected death gripping me now, at last. Duncan murmured sympathetically, hugged me tightly, and kissed my tears away. At length, he told me he loved me, and no one had told me that before, not even my father. He asked me if I trusted him and if I could love him too. And then, at that moment, I surely did. And I'm sure, at that moment, I meant it.

That feeling held for a good three years of his quarterly visits to the ranch. Each time I took him into the mountains. For those three years, I did believe that he was making love to me—that he loved me. But I eventually grew up and opened my eyes.

But his patronage continued to help the ranch survive and prosper.

For twenty-one years I took him into the mountains. Each time he came to the ranch, he'd call ahead to make sure I would be there and free to take him horse riding up in the Blue Ridge.

But not this time. Not for this visit. He had called, yes. My son, Jamie, home from college for the summer, had answered the telephone and told T. Jonas I would be over at the Equestrian Center in Lexington at a horse auction the week he wanted to visit. I didn't necessarily need to go to the auction, but it was time for Jamie to try running the business, making the decisions that needed to be made, on his own.

Jamie and I hadn't gotten along all that well for several years; something had happened—something I'd never learned the reason for—that had cooled him toward me. But this ranch was our family income. He knew that, and he was trying his best to learn the business from me—even while holding me at arms' length. He seemed particularly upset the day Duncan called to set up his next visit.

When I returned from Lexington, my son was nowhere to be seen.

"Where's Jamie?" I asked the first ranch hand I ran up against. "He should be up at reception."

"He's up in the hills with that writer guy, Mr. Zahner. That one you always take up on the parkway with the horses. Jamie was in kind of a fix because the guy showed up and wanted to go riding and taking those photographs of his and you weren't here. He knew Duncan was important, so he went on up into the hills with him to do for him, like you always do."

That was two days ago. Now Duncan was dead. Brought down slung over a horse. The stable workers said Jamie told them it was a riding accident. But I hadn't seen Jamie. I'd been too busy calling Roanoke and making the arrangements. The sheriff over there would be across the mountain and into the valley in a couple of hours and he'd be the one to be asking questions.

But here, in my hand, was the source of a question I hadn't really wanted answered. A photograph at least three decades old. Two men standing by a waterfall up on the Blue Ridge. Duncan on the left and my father, Jamie's grandfather, on the right. And the way Duncan had his arm wrapped around my father, I knew. I suddenly knew. And whatever happened up in those mountains two days ago, Duncan had meant me to see this photograph.

My son. Jamie. It hit me then, and I lurched out of Duncan's room, stopping briefly at the fireplace in the main room to throw the photograph into the flames, and then out into the dusty courtyard. In search of my son. Before the sheriff arrived.

* * * *

Jamie

I saw that photograph. I saw it that first evening he was here, when I went to turn the beds down. I'd already figured he had been doing my dad all these years—not that Dad knew that I knew. But seeing that guy, Duncan, in that old photograph he'd put on his dresser of him with his arm tight around my grandfather—that just set me off. I could have killed him then and there. That photograph—he was flaunting his control and his power. That photograph showed why a big game hunter like Duncan kept coming back to the Blue Ridge to ride horses and take photos of flowers. Both of them. Both my dad and my grandfather: the Zahner men.

I tried to be angry at my dad, but I knew he'd done it to keep the family business going. It's what paid for my college over in Blacksburg; it's what kept food on our table. Duncan had been the ranch's main patron for decades. Everything our family was hinged on Duncan.

His showing up at the ranch unexpectedly while my dad was over in Lexington faced me with a tough decision. He was here even knowing my dad wasn't here. And he wanted to go up into the mountains to ride a horse on a camping trip. So, we saddled up and I took him up to the top of Roanoke Mountain.

I went with the intention of staying my distance, of being polite but standoffish. I didn't want Duncan for a friend—and certainly not for anything more than that—and I was afraid that if I could get within striking distance, I'd kill the man for what he'd done to our family. I couldn't see the point of his fame. I'd read the books and seen the movies done from them, and, yes, he was an engaging, persuasive writer. But that macho male friendship bravado and the constant mining of strength and resolve to take on all comers, whether the scenario was the American West or the battlefields of Iraq, got old pretty fast, I thought.

But the longer I was riding around with him up in at the top of the Blue Ridge, just the two us in sight mostly, with him weaving stories for me in a rich baritone voice that lulled and stroked me to the very quick, the more I could see how he worked on a person. He must have been over sixty by now, but he was still quite a man, the virile, solid, handsome man of power and decisiveness that he wrote about.

The third day we had struck camp in a grove of pines next to a racing stream running down an isolated, sheltering ravine, and then we'd ridden on up toward the ridgeline in search of clear vistas out over the Shenandoah Valley for him to photograph.

We found a mud slide instead. Neither one of us got hurt—and the horses weren't any worse the wear for the slide either. But we were filthy. With a hearty laugh, Duncan challenged me to a horse race down to the crystal-clear little lake the stream running by our camp fed into, and off he roared with another laugh.

It wasn't his horse, so he flew with reckless abandon and was off his steed and in the lake before I got there. When I arrived, he was already splashing around in the water, buck naked and showing off exceptionally well for a man his age. He tossed out a "Don't be a sissy" when I hesitated pulling my jeans off and joining him, and, challenged to the quick, I stripped down and dove into the cold, clear water.

We paddled around a good ten or fifteen feet away from each other, cleaning the mud off ourselves, as he wove another one of his male bonding stories for me—a story of young men starting off in life and those with experience of the world doing so much better than those of limited horizons and narrow views. He told of a young architect, taken under the wing of an older, established master. And how their lives merged and how much their bonding developed the lives and works of both in enriching ways that could never have happened if they'd lived in isolation. I couldn't help but listen to his story in fascination. I aspired to be a writer—I'd shyly told him that several summers ago— and I could see parallels. And I fancied I was drawing those parallels on my own.

"Say, I have an idea," he said, turning laughing eyes in my direction. "Let's have a race across the lake."

"Don't seem hardly fair," I called back to him. "A man your age against a nineteen-year-old athlete who has been ranch handing for the last two months."

"Loser has to both clean and cook the fish tonight," he countered.

That was pretty convincing.

"And the winner gets a shoulder rub right here in the lake, while I try out another story I've been working on," he went on to add.

I thought it was a safe bet, but he, of course, won. I surely didn't like either cleaning or cooking fish, but Duncan had much more at stake than I did. Or did from his perspective, at least.

As I stood in the water close behind him, massaging his back muscles, he was unfolding his idea for a story.

"I've just the bare bones idea as yet," Duncan said, his voice thick with the pleasure of having his sore muscles worked out. "It's about a young man who wants to write about life but who hasn't really experienced life deeply and fully enough for anyone to take notice of what he puts in writing." His voice, his story, were mesmerizing. And I was melting to the words, to him. As the waves were lapping around us, Duncan began murmuring to me in that singsong baritone voice of his, "I know you want to be a writer, Jamie," he was saying. "But do you really think you have the experience and passion for it?"

"Yes, of course," I quickly answered. And then, with more thought. "No . . . No. Probably not. I do find it hard to decide what to write about. And when I do, it often comes out so flat and naïve."

"You know what all of the successful men writers have that you're lacking?" Duncan whispered.

I remained silent, afraid of the answer.

"Bonding," he continued. "That's the success of my writing, Jamie. I write of the most important things—men bonding and taking on the elements together. I live on passion. I need passion for my writing. I can't imagine that you are different. And I'm eternally grateful for all of the inspiration I get from bonding. And I am a giver. I help those who feed my needs."

He let that sink in. I was confused. And frightened. And aroused. I remembered that I had come out here with some sort of resolve, but I couldn't quite focus on what I had resolved to do—or to avoid. His voice. His strong body. His very presence. His slow persistence. That night I slept in his arms, on a blanket, under the stars.

I woke to the sound of the gunshot in the darkness. The fire had gone out long ago. I was alone on the blanket. I stumbled around until I found him, lying beside the racing stream, a smile on his face. The mentor gone, the experience not to be undone. The passion in question. Inspiration surely there, but perhaps never dared to be inked on paper.

I don't know why, but a deep suspicion, almost a realization, hit me at that moment, as I looked down at Duncan's face, smiling a very self-satisfied smile—almost smirk—in death. The relevance not very clear but, at the same time, crystal clear. When my grandfather had died, everyone said it was an accident. In fact, they said it was a accident so often and so distinctly and so loudly that just the saying of it contained the seed of doubting it. He knew the Blue Ridge. He knew you didn't try to drive the parkway in the fog after a blizzard had hit the mountains from the west. He knew. But that's what he had tried and had careened off the road and down the mountainside. Right after one of his trips up into the mountains with Duncan. A Zahner escaping on his own terms?

I was careful in handing the shotgun. There were going to be suspicions enough in any event. There was no reason to have a gun up here in the Blue Ridge. You couldn't

63

hunt up here. I had no idea he'd brought a shotgun along. Motive just below the surface, begging to be set free, hidden, but there in plain sight for any damn fool with half a brain to see. As much on display as that photograph in Duncan's room—now seen as anything but an oversight.

When I had reached the ranch, with the deflated body of Duncan, devoid now of all of its mesmerizing presence and power—its malicious soul—slung unceremoniously over his horse, I heard immediately that my dad had returned from Lexington and also that the sheriff had been called over from Roanoke. It had happened on Roanoke Mountain, so the sheriff in Roanoke claimed jurisdiction. I didn't want to face my dad; I was much more willing to face the sheriff. So, I hid until I saw the sheriff's Jeep nose through the log gate up the road.

In the end, I was saved any suspicion. While the sheriff was driving over from Roanoke, he'd gotten a call from Duncan's doctor in Jackson, Wyoming. Duncan had advanced terminal cancer and had been despondent. The doctor knew Duncan's father had shot himself under similar circumstances, and that worried the doctor.

A doctor's concern. A loose end Duncan hadn't anticipated? That left that damn photograph and my dad. I knew he'd ask what happened between me and Duncan up in the mountains, and I was fully prepared to tell him that nothing had happened, that Duncan had been withdrawn into himself the entire time and hardly spoke to me at all the whole three days. There was no one to dispute me, and I saw no reason to indulge Duncan's last malevolent, controlling plan for domination of the Zahner family.

Now there only remained the photograph. But I couldn't find it. When I went to Duncan's room to search for and destroy it, all of his things had been cleared out already and sent down to Roanoke with his body. In time I almost wondered if it ever had existed at all—almost.

What to Do with Rusty

Aunt Peg's brush with being gassed couldn't have happened at a more inopportune time. Angela had just finished the paperwork on her retirement from the Foreign Service and was still waiting for the movers to arrive at her new house in Crozet, in the eastern shadows of the Blue Ridge Mountains, when she was called to come get Peg's cat, Rusty, and take it to the vet's while Peg was hauled off to the emergency room to have her lungs checked. Peg had turned on the stove in her downtown Charlottesville condo with the pilot light out and had been roused hours later by her old, half-lame cat as she was drifting away. She'd had the presence of mind to throw open all of the doors and windows and get the gas off before tragedy had resulted, so little was actually said—at least to her face—about the state of her faculties. Peg didn't mind going, especially by just drifting off to sleep, but she was mortified at the thought of what might have happened to the others in her apartment building in the process—not the least to her beloved Rusty.

Angela had known that she, as the only relative living nearby, was going to have to face the struggle of Peg giving up her independence and moving into a home sooner or later, but it had been quite inconvenient to have it slap her in the face just now. Angela had just purchased her first home, thanks to a large gift of money from Aunt Peg when the latter had moved out of her house and into a condo. Angela had relocated to Crozet from Falls Church, up in the Washington, D.C., suburbs, which had been her home base between foreign tours for two decades. She came to the rolling hills of central Virginia to get away from the congestion of the city upon retiring and to be closer to Peg in nearby Charlottesville. She had gotten a fairly large house, because she had accumulated a considerable amount of porcelain and crystal during her years in Europe—added to what she had been given by Aunt Peg when the older woman had downsized.

65

Peg's incident with the gas stove had come just while Angela was trying to get settled.

It had been a hard move and transition for Angela. The Foreign Service had been her entire life and had kept her so busy she hadn't developed any outside interests. Now, she was back in the States, completely isolated from the life she had known, and with nothing to do other than perfect her new house and sit on her patio and look up into the Blue Ridge Mountains.

The up side of the new situation with Aunt Peg was that she didn't have to be convinced it was time to let someone else care for her; the down side was that Angela just didn't have time to face this now. But that didn't really prove to be the down side. The gas stove incident had occurred just after Halloween, and Aunt Peg found a retirement home she liked and that had a vacancy before Thanksgiving, but now Rusty had become the stumbling block. Try as either Aunt Peg or Angela might, neither had been able to find an appropriate home for an aging, fat, long-haired cat with a droopy disposition and a lame leg. Aunt Peg had had Rusty since before her husband died, and she couldn't bear to place him with just anybody. Truth be known, she could barely face parting with him at all. He had been the only family she'd had close to her for the last decade.

She couldn't, of course, refer to Rusty as family in Angela's presence. Nonetheless that's how Peg thought of him.

So, it was the middle of December already and, in frustration and with far more feigned willingness than Angela wanted to admit, she had agreed for Aunt Peg to bring Rusty over to her new house for a visit to see if Angela could possibly be able to take the cat in. This Angela most certainly had no intention of doing, but she couldn't be so impolite to Aunt Peg to not be seen as giving it due consideration.

That was what had brought the two—the three, if you counted Rusty—to this crucial day. Aunt Peg bustled into Angela's living room and perched in a rocking chair right next to the Christmas tree that was decorated with delicate crystal ornaments Angela had picked up around Europe over a good many years. This was the first time she'd been able to put them all on display at one time.

Rusty huddled, trembling, in Aunt Peg's lap, knowing that something significant was afoot, but also knowing he would not be happy about what that might be.

Aunt Peg was a nervous wreck. She knew this was Rusty's last chance at a home where she might still be able to visit him from time to time. She was trying her best to show him off to good effect in front of Angela, but she was failing miserably, and Rusty wasn't helping at all. He just buried his face in the bosom of her dress and hissed at Angela whenever she came near, showing no sign of understanding what was what—what Peg was trying to do for him.

After an initial stilted conversation, Angela excused herself to put the tea on in the kitchen. She had just lifted one of her favorite porcelain tea pots down from the shelf on which it was displayed with a good many others like it, when she heard the sound of shattering glass from the living room. The unexpected sound made her drop her tea pot into the kitchen sink, where it shattered into six jagged pieces.

Tears bubbled up into Angela's eyes as she rushed back into the living room. There, she found several of the crystal ornaments from the tree on the floor and the tree still swaying a bit, as Rusty hopped back into Aunt Peg's lap and buried his muff in an opening in her cardigan sweater.

Aunt Peg was speechless, just staring at Angela in misery as she entered the room. Angela bubbled over with rage and hurt, and she knew that she would lash out at her aunt if she were forced to say anything at all at this point. All of this work to get her house just right and all of these beautiful things she had accumulated, and they were shattering around her because of some old cat that should just be put down.

Angela mumbled something that couldn't really be interpreted to mean anything at all and, fetching a broom and dustpan, quickly swept up the broken crystal and marched back toward the kitchen.

"Oh, I'm so sorry," Aunt Peg finally managed to say to her niece's back. "And what was that I heard from the kitchen? Something else broken?"

The question just hung in the air. Angela was already through the door into the kitchen, letting it swing shut behind her. She made a brutal jab at the trash can with the dustpan and emptied possibly $200 of once-fine, but now worthless, glass into the trash. Then she marched over to the sink, gathered up the porcelain shards, and threw them away as well.

She stood at the sink, gripping the edge with her hands, her knuckles turning white. She slowly counted down from fifty, regulating her breath with her counting. The radio was playing, and she concentrated on the words of "The Little Drummer Boy" while fighting for control. It very likely was the first time she'd ever concentrated on those words.

"I have no gift to bring . . . That's fit to give the King."

She now felt calm enough to resume making a pot of tea. She reached up for a replacement tea pot for the one that had broken and, for the first time, realized just how many porcelain tea pots she had. She counted them slowly. She had nine porcelain tea pots, not counting the broken one. For some reason, this made Angela giddy, and she started to laugh. It took her more than a minute to regain control of herself, and then she made the tea and opened the cupboard to find tea cups. She saw that she had tea cups by the dozens. She had tea cups to go with each of those porcelain tea pots. She found the ones that went with the tea pot she was using and arranged these and a sugar bowl and some cookies on one of several trays she found in the cupboard under the sink.

As she was arranging the tray, Angela recalled the look her aunt had given her when she'd entered the living room to view the broken crystal. It had been a look of fear and despair and of defeat. And Angela remembered how that old, lame cat—the cat that had been her aunt's sole companion for over a decade and that had pawed at his mistress to get her attention as her condo was filling with gas—had retreated to Aunt Peg's lap and how Aunt Peg had sheltered him, desperately hugging him to her in her despair.

Angela stopped fussing with the tray and steeled herself for what she had to do next. She counted to twenty this time until her nerves had calmed. Then, she picked up the tray and marched back into the living room.

Aunt Peg still had that miserable look on her face as Angela put the tray down on the coffee table and sat down in a chair closely facing her aunt.

"Angela, I know—"

"Aunt Peg, I can't take your cat."

Peg's lips were trembling and her eyes were misting. It took her a moment to compose herself enough to speak.

"I know, my dear. I'm so sorry. All these beautiful things. I know you can't have a cat like Rusty here." She was so close to tears she could barely get the words out. "But I've tried everything I can think of. I just wished they'd let me have him at the home. I guess there's nothing else to do. I'll just have to have him—"

"Oh, shush, Aunt Peg. Don't even say it. I mean that I can't take your cat from you at all. I can see what you mean to each other. I'll take Rusty, but only if you'll come with him. There's plenty of room here. I don't have to have all of this stuff out where the cat will stumble over it. I'm lonely too and haven't any notion of what to do with my life now. You've asked me several times what I want for Christmas. I've never answered, because I already have too much of everything in this house. But what I don't have in this house is a family. Can I have you and Rusty as my family, living here with me, as a present for my first Christmas here?"

Angela liked the look that now materialized on her aunt's face much better than the trapped look she had seen earlier, and she knew she was making the right decision.

Timing Out

"Guess what, Mom? We went all the way to Baghdad. Straight to Baghdad. Racing in our Humvees. No Problem. Whooie. Me and my buds are having the time of our lives. Ain't that great, Mom?"

"Yes, Craig, that's great. Does that mean you're coming right home?" Laura tried her best not to let her voice show the depth of her concern or her mixed feelings about this whole military deal.

"You shoulda seen 'em wavin', Mom. They all came out on the street to welcome us. We're freeing them, Mom. It'll all be over in no time. You shoulda seen them waving."

"That's wonderful, son. Ummm, do you think you'll be getting home by August? Lonny at the garage will have to get out for the harvest, and Mr. Dickerson was saying—"

"Gee, I don't know, Mom. There's word a few units will have to stay on for a while. We might—"

"You know what I can't quite understand. You're in the National Guard—what's the National Guard doin' so far from the nation? That's what I wanna know." Laura nearly burst out in tears. She'd coached herself to not go off like this. Certainly not at Craig for the few moments she'd get to talk with him from so far away. She knew her time with him on the phone was precious.

She took a drag on her cigarette to calm herself and then recoiled from that and tossed the cigarette in the sink. She'd been told to get rid of that crutch, as if that mattered any more. And she'd done all right—until Craig got sent off and that fighting had started.

"It's just that Mr. Dickerson can't hold your job at the garage down in Luray forever, Craig. And you worked so hard to get it. It's just such bad timing. I—"

"Sorry, I gotta go, Mom. Guys are standing in line, and we have a time limit. You should get on the Internet, Mom. That's how the soldiers out here are keeping connected with their families. See Jim. He can get you fixed up."

"Sure, son. I'll see Jim—"

"Gotta go, Mom. Give my love to Charlene, will ya? Haven't gotten an e-mail from her yet."

"Sure, but hold on. There's something I need to tell you. I—"

"Gotta ring off, Mom. All the best. It's really great what we're doin' out here, Mom. Bye now."

Laura lowered the receiver with a trembling hand, turned to the sink, fished out the still-smoldering cigarette, and took another deep, evil drag.

"Bye, son. I needed to tell you about the cancer they found, though." This was spoken aloud and full of biting bitterness to the silent, dreary kitchen in the old log and clapboard farmhouse up the dirt road in Jordan Hollow, a fold in the Blue Ridge Mountains just to the east of the Shenandoah Valley town of Luray. Tired lace curtains, split linoleum on the floor, and traces of sunlight on the warped cabinets shining through the chinks in the plaster between the logs. Still, somehow, she felt better, strangely comforted, for having said it out loud, for having named it—if only to herself for now.

* * * *

"He what?"

"I'm sorry, Craig. Mr. Dickerson had to let your job go to a new mechanic he brought in from over in Harrisonburg. He said he tried to hold it for you as long as he could, but he ran out of time; he's got a business to try to keep open. Life goes on here, you know; it doesn't hold still here for Iraq."

Silence.

"Do you think you'll be home for Christmas, Craig? This is really taking too—"

"Don't know, Mom. I doubt it. It's stringing out a little longer than they figured. There's a little resistance. But we're going to win. We're going to do this thing."

A short pause, with Laura turning away from the receiver so Craig couldn't hear her heavy sigh. And her hacking cough.

Then Craig again. "Mom, I'm wondering if Charlene's having trouble with her computer. My e-mails don't seem to be going through. And have you talked to Jim about getting you set up? I sure do miss you, Mom."

Laura couldn't breathe. She had to sit down. They told her there'd be moments like this in this stage. But she didn't think this was the sickness. At least not the physical sickness. She needed to see her boy, to hold him in her arms—the visceral need of connection. He couldn't know what "missing" really was—not like she knew; not like this monster that had a grip on her was forcing her to understand.

"No, I haven't talked to Jim yet. A computer's a little out of my budget at the—"

"Haven't you gotten the checks they were supposed to be sending you, Mom?"

"Yes, yes, of course." How to tell him where the money from the checks was going. She'd tried to tell him the last time, but this just wasn't the way—or the right time. Not across the miles like this. And not now. She'd been watching the news. He couldn't be having that on his mind just now. Maybe later, when everything over there was settling down. As surely it would. Sometime soon. Surely.

"Mom? Mom? You sound kinda hoarse. You got a cold or something? You keep the heat going in that old shed now, Mom. Cold weather's setting in and . . . well, I don't know how you can take the winters there anyway."

"Don't you worry about me, Craig. Just you stay safe and come home. If they have any Christmas leave on offer, grab it . . . for me . . . for my sake. OK? It's all I want for Christmas."

"Yeah, sure, Mom. That'd be great. Now, about Charlene—"

Laura held the phone to her ear for the longest time, willing it not to have gone dead. Desperate to hear his voice again, staying in connection, even if only over a phone line at great distance.

* * * *

"She what?"

"Charlene got married a week ago Saturday. I'm sorry, son. I thought she would have told you. It was that new mechanic at Dickerson's garage—the one who took your job there. I spoke to her at the church for a minute afterward. She said time was flyin', and she couldn't just put her life on hold forever."

Silence.

"I'm real sorry. I know you shouldn't be hearing anything that will get you down right now. I read the papers. I know you're having it rough there. Believe me, I'd do all I could not to be conveying bad news from home."

If only he knew how far she'd gone with that, she thought, wrapping her coat tight around her chest. She'd used the last of the wood two days ago, and it was fixing to snow tomorrow. It was the middle of the night now and there was a ring around the moon. That always meant there'd be a storm. But it had come down to a choice between treatments, food, or heat. She'd managed two of them, at least. Oh, God, why couldn't her son be coming home? What in the hell were they doing over there anyway?

"Well . . . I guess you're not going to get that computer and learn how to connect to e-mails, are you?" It was almost an accusation, his disappointment knifing down the phone lines and slicing into her heart. A flash of anger and hurt shot through her too. She hadn't had electricity for a month, so e-mails were sort of a bad joke just now. She'd laugh if she weren't trying so hard to stifle a sob. Instead, she jagged into a coughing fit. It wasn't his fault; he just wanted to have whatever connection they were to be allowed. It just wasn't the connection she needed herself.

"Mom? Mom? Did you get that cold I told you not to get?"

"Yes, I guess I did. I guess I just can't do anything right when you're not here. Can't you come—?"

"Ah, shit, Mom. They're motioning me to give up the phone. Time's up, Mom. Merry Christmas, ya hear? Time's up. Love ya. Bye."

Click.

Time's up. Time's up. Yes, just about right, Laura thought bitterly. And then she did break down . . . into open-mouthed, hunched-against-the-counter, see-your-frozen-breath icy sobs, huddled there, wrapped in her winter coat in the "warmest" room in her cabin, soon overtaken by wracking coughs.

* * * *

Moving up the road into the hollow from the bus stop as fast as he could in eight inches of crunchy snow. His ragged breath steaming, thinking wild thoughts, searching for the chimney of the old farmhouse. Craig was cold, nearly frozen stiff. He'd thought it was cold in Baghdad that January. But Baghdad wasn't anything like here in the winter. He'd been gone too long. His body had forgotten how to adjust to the cold of a Blue Ridge Mountain winter—assuming anyone ever could.

He had to see the chimney, to see the curling smoke of home, to know it wasn't as bad as he feared. Phil from down at the store had called him and told him it was bad with his mother, and, in shock, he'd gone to his sergeant, and they'd furloughed him home. They'd said they could give him a little time; all he needed to do was ask. Time. A little time.

There, wasn't that the house? But, no, it couldn't be. That one looked abandoned. But, yes, yes, that was the house. How could he have forgotten so quickly? Home.

But, there wasn't any smoke coming out of the chimney.

Craig tried moving faster in the snow drifts and only managed to fall down and get snow inside his boots.

Hurry, hurry, hurry. And then just sit and ponder and wonder and succumb to the reproofs. The house was empty, deserted, and cold as an ice floe and had obviously been that way for some time—a solitary Arctic ice floe. Craig sat there

74

in the kitchen, huddled in his coat, feeling the snow melting, ice cold, through his socks. Looking at the tired lace curtains and the split linoleum and the warped cabinets, but not really seeing them.

Time had run out. She wasn't here. Why hadn't she told him on the phone? His eyes focused on the telephone. But, of course, she'd tried to tell him. He knew that now, now that he concentrated for the first time on what she had been saying—and what she hadn't been saying. She'd sat right here where he was sitting, talking to him on the phone, trying to tell him how fleeting time was. She had been reaching out, wanting to touch him, and all he'd been able to think of was playing savior soldier half a world away and wondering why she couldn't be bothered to get on the Internet and connect with him. Connections could time out just like that while you're off crunching up time to little or no effect.

Craig snapped alert to the ringing of the telephone.

"Craig, that you? Phil from down at the store. Hoped you'd be there. Your mom's down here in Luray at the house. We came up there and brought her down last night. She hadn't told anyone just how bad it was up there. Get yourself on over here, boy. You ask me, it's time you guys stopped spinning your wheels over there and were brought on home for good. There's enough needs doin' and savin' and savoring right here."

Craig let out a sob and lurched for the door. Time. Just a little more time, probably. But every minute precious and fleeting now.

Molly's Picnic Table

"It's so peaceful out here in the shadow of the Blue Ridge. It will be hard to leave."

"Yes, it is," I answered. I didn't address the "hard to leave" part as I was hoping to buy this slice of heaven from the Talleys. And Molly Talley appeared as if, with half a notion, she'd march down the road and pull the "For Sale" sign out of the ground. Her voice was pleasant enough, but she was sitting in a defensive stance there at the picnic table, arms crossed tight under ample bosoms and wispy salt-and-pepper hair frizzed in strands around her thick-jowled face that had defied her attempts to put them up in the bun at the back of her head.

"The views of the mountains from here are spectacular," I added, trying to warm up the conversation. Neither of the Talleys seemed much for chitchat.

"Yes, I suppose," Mrs. Talley answered, squinting at me through eyeglass lens as thick as Coke bottle bottoms.

I could have kicked myself. The Talleys were being quite hospitable on this visit—almost as if they wanted to say yes. And I seemed unable to say the right things to push them over the edge.

"It's been fifty-three years since we took up homing in this house," Molly said, with a sigh. "Ain't that so, Tom?"

I looked over at Molly's husband, Tom, a gawky sort of silent gray man with a plaid shirt and suspenders on worn jeans, who, if he'd turned sideways to me, would have disappeared altogether. As it was, he was only half there, anyway, concentrating on chewing on his wad of tobacco. Rather than looking at either of us, he was staring at the old tractor sitting off under the nearby hickory tree as if he was already back on it and turning rows in the small patch of garden on the slope off to the west, under the late afternoon shadow of the Blue Ridge Mountains. Tom nodded in agreement with Molly, however, so I supposed he was still hanging onto the edge of the conversation.

"Tom inherited this piece of land and the house from his father, Tom Senior. It was passed on to him by his father, Willie Talley . . . that right, Tom? No, tisn't, is it? Wally. His name was Wally. If Tom and me wasn't gettin' too old to get groceries in—and if we had someone to pass it on to—we would be astayin'."

"Yes, it is a lovely, peaceful setting, Mrs. Talley. I wouldn't want to change hardly anything. I've been looking for something exactly like this for a couple of years now."

That was the truth—both that it was a lovely setting and that I'd been looking for exactly this for two years, ever since I'd moved to Charlottesville and started working for the University Press. Charlottesville was fine, but I wanted to write in the free time I had, and there was just too much going on in the town. Soon after I got to Virginia, I started looking in the surrounding countryside for someplace perfect to live and write in peace. I knew I wanted to have a view of the mountains and to be away from the bustle of traffic and the lure of concerts, festivals, and activities.

I'd been up Bucks Mountain Road, up toward the Blue Ridge, several times in the past year. And I had seen and admired the Talleys' place before I saw the "For Sale" sign go up on its front lawn. I immediately tracked the Realtor down, and this was the second visit I'd paid to the Talleys to work on them to pass the place on to me. The Realtor had said that the couple desperately needed to move into a nursing home—especially Tom, who was having heart and other health issues—but that they had no concept of selling as soon as possible to whoever could swing the mortgage. Real estate wasn't moving any faster in Albemarle County than any place else in the nation in these economic down times. But so far the Talleys hadn't let that hurry them along to the inevitable.

The house was perfect for me—a brick two over two at the front, which must have dated back to the nineteenth century, and a wooden addition off the back, housing a kitchen and laundry room on the ground floor and a large bath and storage room above. The brick section was over an English basement, and one of the rooms down there would be perfect for the Virginia wines I was becoming addicted to.

My exercise equipment could go in the other. The house sat on a rise at the front, with about forty feet of flat backyard, which then rose again in oak and pine forest up one of the slopes of Bucks Mountain. There were views of mountains—looming right overhead—in all directions except the southeast. Charlottesville was only a twenty-minute drive away—but it was a world away in bustle and traffic.

There was an open porch off the back of the brick section and beside the kitchen. I had plans already to enclose that as a sun porch and use it for my study, where I'd write facing the blue mists coming off the mountains to the west. But I wouldn't tell the Talleys that. I didn't want to queer any possibility of a deal.

"We wouldn't want any changes," Molly was saying. "We'd want family to see the house just the way it's always been when they come by. We've heard of stories where people went to look for the house they growed up in and drove around and around without recognizing anything from their childhood. I find that kinda sad."

I didn't think the Talleys had any family left to care about in that vein. My understanding was that this was the basic issue here—that they needed care now and there were no relations to provide it. I was probably thinking too hard on this, though, and not enough about walking on eggs in the conversation, or I wouldn't have said what I next did.

"I was thinking of putting in a swimming pool. Probably right here where this picnic table slab is, but it would be hidden from view from the road, from in front of the . . ."

The change in the expression on Molly Talley's wide, deeply lined face brought me to a stop. "Oh, shit," I thought. "Now I've shot all of my cajoling up to now and will have to backtrack. Good thing I didn't mention the sun porch."

Molly looked horrified, and she was struggling to raise her bulk up from the picnic bench.

But I realized that she wasn't looking at me; she was looking past me. I turned my head to see that her husband, Tom, had keeled over onto the top of the picnic table, his face buried in the red and white-checked vinyl table cloth

Molly had spread there when we sat down with our glasses of mint iced tea.

* * * *

"I want to thank you for seein' that we got down to the hospital," Molly said to me as she stood from the chair on the other side of the bed they'd put Tom in. She was clutching a huge black purse in front of her as if she was shielding herself from the world, her thick legs rising up from black nurse's shoes spreading wide like some harbor colossus. She hadn't taken off the white frilly apron she'd been wearing while we were sitting at her picnic table, but she'd grabbed a pillbox hat with a little black net on it and perched it on her head as we left. No doubt wearing a hat when she went out had been so ingrained in her during her mother's generation that she would have felt naked without it. I took her thank-you and her rising from the chair as my cue to leave.

But after I'd murmured something to her in response that neither one of us expected to be more than politeness and also stood, she surprised me.

"Please," she said, a bit hesitant, "if you don't mind, could you stay and sit with Tom for a few minutes? I need to check with them at the nurses' stand, and I do believe I need some coffee. This has all been a bit distressing."

"Yes, of course," I answered, sitting back down. There was nothing I wanted less to do than to sit and listen to Tom's ragged breathing—holding my own breath until I was sure he'd taken his next one. But I was resigned to staying a bit longer. It wasn't to stay on anyone's good side to convince them to sell their house to me—it was because my mother's generation had taught me more than to wear a hat when I went out. It was the right thing to do.

I planned to doze a bit while Molly was gone, but soon after she left, I looked at Tom and realized that his eyes were open and he was looking at me intently, almost wildly. He lifted a hand, and I recognized the gesture as a request that I come closer. I leaned forward in my chair, my face

79

close to his. He clutched the collar of my shirt in a grip that was surprisingly strong and dragged me even closer.

"Don't let Tom at her. Tain't her fault," I heard him mutter. Or at least I thought that's what he said.

"Sorry, what did you say?"

"Tim would know what to do. He wouldn't let him at 'er. Nothin' she could have done about it anyways."

"Tom, are you OK? You're in the hospital. Do you want me to call for a nurse?"

"It's gotta stop. It's not her; it's him. He's gotta stop."

I repeated the offer to ring for a nurse, but Tom had loosened his hold on my shirt and had laid his head back on the pillow. His eyes were open briefly, staring straight up to the ceiling, and then they glazed over, closed, and his ragged breathing took over again.

I leaned back in my chair, trembling. It wasn't so much what he'd said that made me shudder as it was his wild-eyed countenance when he'd said it. Tom Talley had been almost completely silent the two times I'd visited their house—almost transparent, barely there, although whenever his wife, Molly, had invoked his name, he'd nod his head like he was following the conversation.

"He was awake for a moment—but just briefly," I told Molly Talley when she returned to the room. She was carrying two foam cups of steaming coffee, one of which she handed to me. So, I couldn't flee yet. She'd brought me coffee; I'd have to sit there and drink it before I made my excuses and left—my mother's generation's rules again.

I had to hold the cup with both hands to keep it from spilling. I was still disconcerted by the little episode with Tom.

"Did he say anything you could understand?" she asked as she heaved her bulk back into the chair on the other side of the bed. It was spoken nonchalantly, but I was watching her as she said it, and she was looking with noticeable concern at the now-inert form of her husband.

"I didn't understand much; something about Tom and Tim—but he talked of Tom in the third person. Rather strange."

"Umm, yes," Molly answered, "Yes, well. You sure he didn't say John?"

"He might have. But it was quite strange. It was like he was someone else altogether."

"Well, Tom's been like that for a while. It's why we haven't really gone out for some time. He's sort of more than one person. Doc said something about 'demented,' but neither Tom nor I liked the sound of that, so we haven't been back to Doc for a while."

"'Dementia.' Maybe that's what he said—John," I responded. "Dementia's sort of an illness; there's nothing really bad about it—just something that causes people to become confused."

"I suppose."

"So, does Tom sometimes talk about himself as if he's someone else—and talk about a John?"

"I suppose . . . sometimes."

"But is there a Tim in his life too?"

Molly looked at me—at first with suspicion and then her countenance relaxed. I'd almost describe it as imploding in on herself and surrendering to exhaustion. She sipped on her coffee for a moment and then looked at me again. Her eyes now looked imploring, as if she had a burden to lay down.

I regret to say that I seem to have that effect on people. They often tell me things about their lives I don't really want to hear. But here I sat, my coffee still too hot to drink, trapped in politeness.

"Tom's brother is named Tim. Identical twins they are—but as different in temperament as night and day."

"Oh, I was under the impression that neither one of you had living relatives."

"Well, we don't know about Tim. He was there one day and then gone the next. Seven years ago now, in April. But then Tim was like that. He was Navy. We were never sure when he'd show up or how long he'd stay. He moved as it pleased him. He was a pleasure to be around, though."

From this, I got an inkling that perhaps Tom hadn't always been that much of a pleasure to be around. I didn't say anything, though. I didn't have to because Molly wanted to talk now.

"Last time he was home, though, he made a big difference. I don't know how much longer I could have gone on with Tom. Tim really turned him around."

"Umm," I responded, sipping my coffee, wanting it— and me—to be gone.

"That's when I got that picnic table we were sittin' at. I love that picnic table. Not just because it's so pleasant there, but also because of the turnaround it meant."

"Oh?" This time I was paying more attention. She had my attention now. Something about this . . .

"Yes. It all happened right then—Tim leaving and Tom changing and me getting' that nice picnic table—after me fallin' down the stairs and haven' to go up to Doc's in the evening and get my arm set and put in a cast."

We sat there in silence for a few minutes. I didn't feel much like silence, though. My heart was beating fast, and I felt like screaming inside, without really knowing why. I looked over at Tom, laying there so peaceful. The doctor had been quite guarded about his condition when we came in. I thought he was trying to tell Molly not to expect much of anything good, but she had that big, black purse shielding herself from him, and I wasn't sure she was understanding. Now, when I looked at Tom, I wondered for the first time who I was looking at.

"When I got home, Tom and Tim were at it. Land, I don't think they'd ever had words and stomping around like that before as long as I'd been married to Tom. They simmered down when I got home, though. And Tim was special nice to me and helped me up the stairs to the bedroom. He had some fool idea, though, that I kept tellin' him was just not right. But he didn't yell at me like he was doin' at Tom."

"Some idea?" I asked.

"Yes, indeed. He had some idea that I hadn't fallen down the stairs. But he didn't know how clumsy I could be— and not being able to see much of anything—even with these here glasses. But I was just a clumsy dodo in those days."

"In those days?"

"Yes, not so much recently. And Tom changed too. Right there and then. The next morning Tim was gone, but Tom was suddenly a whole new man. Cheery and thoughtful. That fight he'd had with Tim must have done him a world of good. That very morning, he asked me if I'd like a picnic table out there near the hickory tree, where we could see the mountains all around. And, of course, I said I would. We'd always had a picnic table out back at my family's place. I'd even mentioned it a couple of times to Tom, but he hadn't taken the hint then. But he sure took the bull by the horns on that day. Went right down to Southern States and got the table and benches and the concrete mix. Made the slab himself, he did."

With that Molly seemed to wind down and sat there reminiscing about how she'd gotten the picnic table she'd always wanted.

I, however, was tied up in knots. I didn't know what to think—what to say. I looked down at Tom. He seemed to be withering away right before my eyes. I was happy then that Molly had been talking and not seeing what I could see.

"Molly. What about Molly?" I thought. I didn't even know if I had the right—or the justification—to think what I thought. But I couldn't let it go.

I took a sip of the coffee. Now cold already. When had it changed from steaming to cold? Molly hadn't been talking that long. I drank it anyway, trying to decide what, if anything to say, to do. Building up strength to do what I knew I had to do or I'd always wonder, worry.

"I'm sorry," I began, building up strength. "I didn't know what the picnic table meant to you. I'm sorry about what I said about a swimming pool. If I buy the house, of course I'll do without a pool or locate it elsewhere. I'll keep the picnic table right where it is."

"Oh, land, I don't think it matters anymore," Molly answered. "You can have the house; I know it's the nursing home for us—for me—now. And you can do what you like with the picnic table. I got my enjoyment out of it."

She was looking directly at me. No sign of worry or distress in her eyes—at least not about the picnic table.

"She doesn't know," I thought, with a great sigh of relief, feeling all of the organs in my body sinking back into their proper alignment. But then, I didn't know either. Not really.

What I did know, though, was that I'd find someplace else to dig my swimming pool.

How Big the Ocean?

"Just don't—"

"Screw it up again?" I nearly yelled into the cell phone. I wasn't angry; it was just hard to talk over the crying in the backseat. I actually laughed.

"I didn't mean that," Helen answered in a wounded voice. "It's just that you can be so . . . so . . ."

"Flighty?" I offered, accompanied by a snort. I turned my head and told the two girls back there to pipe down, but that had no effect at all. You can't reason with a Siamese cat being subjected to something it didn't choose—especially when it had a companion willing to sympathize and harmonize with it.

"Sandra!" Helen said. I always knew when she'd had enough. She called me Sandra rather than Sandi.

"I'm just kidding you," I responded. "I know you've pulled strings—yet again—to get me this job interview. I think the world of you for doing this, and I promise I'll get there on time . . . if I can."

"S-a-n-d-r-a . . . are those children I hear crying in the background? Have you gone off track again?"

"Sorry, hon, gotta go. I think my exit is coming up." I shut down the phone and argued with myself on whether this was the exit for the Siamese rescue center east of Madison. It was, but I hadn't decided that in time, and now I'd have to go to the next exit and turn back. And I was already running late for getting to that interview. Darn!

It was great that Helen had gotten me this interview. She'd always been the steady one. We'd been inseparable through seminary, where we were both preparing to be ministers of education, but then Helen had gone steadily up, and I'd had to row double time just to stay on the surface of the water. "You'll never make it anywhere, if you don't apply yourself and find good jobs in churches," Helen had constantly said. And she was right, I hadn't gone anywhere.

Helen had moved up quickly in her jobs—saved souls and gathered accolades. And I had yet to be placed in a church job at all. I was a failure as a Christian. My mother had been diagnosed with Alzheimer's right when I was being anointed, which had taken up my time in being with her as much as possible, and as hard as Helen had tried to get me into church positions since my mother passed, I was still on the outside looking in.

Helen would have had a fit if she'd known that I had agreed to get these cats to the Siamese rescue center on my way to this job interview she had gotten for me in a big church in a university town. But the center was on my way— well, not more than fifty miles out of the way—and we were coming on to Christmas. This was high season for placing cats in homes. These little girls in the backseat needed every opportunity possible to find a home by Christmas.

As it turned out, either my maps weren't too helpful or I was busy cajoling the cats when I should have been looking at the road, because it took far too long to find the rescue center, and then I had to move my old rattletrap beyond its endurance to make Charlottesville in time. I headed for the center of town, knowing the church was near there, and after circling around for a while, I found, by driving right up to the edge of it and running out of road, that they had bricked over their main street to make a nifty walking mall.

I never asked, but Shantay must have really thought I was a sight when she came upon me as I sat there in my dusty Civic, where the asphalt was divided from red brick by a couple of metal barriers, watching the minutes between where I was and where I needed to be fritter away. I was looking bewilderedly at the flickering fairy lights in the trees on the pedestrian mall in the waning light of day when Shantay hefted her ample bosoms on the passenger windowsill and scrunched her ebony face down to where she could look me in the eye. Her hair radiated in gray and black wisps from a wrinkled, expressive face that managed to display humor and slight concern simultaneously.

Sensing her presence, I looked up into the face of a woman who looked just about as far down on her luck as possible, and every good intention I had of making that job interview in seven more minutes was shattered when, after I'd rolled the passenger door window down, she put on a sympathetic expression and said, "You all right, honey? Do you need help?"

She was asking me if I needed help.

Shantay—who had been quick to tell me that was her name—was wheezing so hard when she asked this that I was bewildered at how she could help me. From what I could see, the only reason she was half standing was because she was propped against the side of my car. And yet she seemed to be genuinely concerned about me.

I told her what church I was looking for, and she wrinkled up her nose but did turn and point up the hill behind me—where the church quite obviously was perched.

"Thanks," I said. "But why the hesitancy?"

"Not my first choice of churches," Shantay answered through hard breathing. "I used to sleep up there under their portico, but then they put in steel grates to keep us from doin' that. Usually sleep over by the library now. There's room over there, if—"

"No thanks," I answered. "I have a room reserved for the night. In fact—"

It was an instantaneous decision, one of those flighty acts of mine that always sent Helen into mumbling and grumbling. But it was getting dark, and I suddenly wasn't so sure I wanted to work at that particular church anyway.

It was getting to where it was decidedly cool at night even here in the South—we were entering the Christmas season, and Shantay was looking pretty delicate despite her massive bulk. So I told her I'd love to share her graciously offered space with her, but I already had two rooms reserved down at the Days Inn, and I couldn't see why one of them should go to waste, so why didn't she take one of those rooms for the night as my guest and, if she would, perhaps she could come to dinner with me—that I really hated to eat alone.

87

Shantay said nothing when I went into the motel office, praying all the way that they had two rooms available, which they did. I got the impression while we ate that evening at a Greek restaurant across the road and toward the university that it had been some time since Shantay had gotten a good meal. Luckily, I'd asked at the motel reception desk for a nearby, inexpensive restaurant that served good food, and the desk clerk had come up with a winner in all departments. We didn't out eat what I had space for on a credit card.

She was a real Christmas gift to me. She was a great conversationalist and could conjure up a basic truth faster and clearer than anyone who had taught me at the seminary. She was always ready to laugh even when she knew it would finish off in a painful cough—a cough I had heard too often before—and knew where that would lead to soon. I wished that everyone could face the inevitable as well as Shantay was doing.

We got into talking about Christmas and Christmas gifts, and I asked her what she had always wanted and never gotten. She sat and thought and chewed and coughed for a long minute.

"Well, you know, I've had about everything I needed in life. But if I had a choice of a Christmas present, I do believe I'd ask to see the ocean. I've never seen that and I'm told it's just over yonder. And I'm told it's pretty big. Yes, I think I'd like to see the ocean before I die."

I didn't like the look she gave when the subject of death came up, so I quickly said that I had never seen the Atlantic myself and had, in fact, left the Midwest with the intention of seeing the Eastern Shore and was just then on my way to getting that done.

Toward late afternoon of the next day, Shantay and I pulled up next to the sand at the poorer end of Virginia Beach. Shantay was a lot weaker by then than she had been the previous day, and I now understood why I had thrown that wheelchair into the trunk of the Civic back in Indianapolis after looking after Mrs. Bates to the end rather than leaving it behind as the neighbors had suggested.

As I wheeled Shantay out onto the sand as far as the wheelchair could go, she was giving off little clucking sounds and an occasional "Oh, my." It eventually got dark enough that we could barely see the water, but still Shantay sat there and stared out to sea, watching the effect of the sunset on the water as the sun sank below the horizon behind us. After a long stretch of silence, she gave a larger sigh than normal, trailing off into a disturbing cough, and allowed as how it was a very nice ocean but not quite as big as she had thought it would be. The deep smile lines on her face, however, belied any disappointment she might have expressed.

I was able to find a small, rundown cottage just off the beach that, along with a few others, rented by the day. Shantay died three days later, but we had managed to get out on the sand every one of those days.

I called Helen to tell her I was sorry I had missed the job interview but something had come up and I hadn't made it there.

Helen wasn't too pleased at first. She said she knew I'd missed the appointment, because she'd talked to the minister at the church. She lit into me something fierce—the usual declarations of how I was just floating around and wasting my life on minutia and had wasted all that training to be a minister to people and how it was impossible to understand how the two of us could have turned out so different.

In the end, though, she sighed and said, "Reverend Claxton said they'd hold the interviews open if you could make it in the next day or two. I told him how good you'd be in the job—and that's the truth, Sandi. You'd be such an inspiration and a rock for people to cling to if you'd just settle down and apply yourself. And the reverend said he could hold off on a decision for two days. So, could you—?"

"I'll do what I can to be there, Helen. And again, thanks for trying to help me." I felt myself tearing up when I clicked off. Helen was such a good soul, and she was trying so hard with me. I knew I was a major disappointment to her. I just couldn't help myself.

It took all of the next day to make final arrangements for Shantay. While I was packing to leave, I heard one real corker of a domestic fight going on in the cottage next to ours. I can't say I was surprised. The young couple and their two toddlers had been in the cottage when we arrived, and they obviously had not been having a pleasant vacation. The man was a drinker, and the woman had skittered around like a frightened rabbit for days trying to keep the kids quiet and out of his way. But even when she had taken them out on the sand and settled them into making sandcastles, he would weave his way out there, scream at her about something that hadn't been done right, and set both kids off before returning to the cottage, jumping into his Camaro, and roaring off until late in the night.

When I carried my bag out to the Civic to leave for that interview at the Charlottesville church, his Camaro was kicking up dust once more, and it was loaded down so heavy I could tell the man didn't intend to come back. I was just closing the trunk when the woman staggered out of her cottage and collapsed into a weeping heap on the steps. She looked beat up pretty bad.

As I walked over toward her, all I could think of was that I wasn't going to be making it to that interview in time again. In spite of all the good intentions in the world, I had once again proven to be a big disappointment to Helen.

Good Customer

"Here comes your good customer, Trixie. Right on the dot. Just remember that I've got him the first week in May. We'll see if he's as good a tipper for me as he is for you."

"I don' know, Becky. Maybe I'll just have to come back into town every morning just to serve Mr. Turner his breakfast."

At 8:15 a.m. sharp, just like for the last seven years, Mr. Turner appeared from around the corner, walking briskly toward The Nook restaurant.

"Oh, Gawd. There's that girl again in her motor contraption. She's going to do some serious harm if she don't slow down." Trixie didn't want Mr. Turner to wind up on the disabled list rather than sitting at his favorite table for his usual. But it looked like he was safe for another day. He had seen the girl coming down the bricked walking street and had turned to greet her. But she was staring off through the trees and across the Mall at one of those young business-suit types and had barely missed Mr. Turner in passing. Good, Trixie thought. She had enough on her mind not to have her schedule thrown off by Mr. Turner missing his breakfast.

Trixie couldn't imagine why Mr. Turner had become one of her breakfast regulars here at The Nook, as he owned his own restaurant up away on the Downtown Mall. They didn't serve breakfast there, but that didn't mean they wouldn't serve it to their owner.

He shuffled in the door; pressed those big hands, with those long fingers, on the tabletop; and eased his considerable bulk down into a little round-bottomed chair that hardly looked strong enough to hold him. Just the imposing—she once would have thought, intimidating—appearance of him reminded Trixie of just how amazing it was that she now looked forward to his appearance every weekday morning. Where she had been raised up in the hollows between Crozet and the Shenandoah National Parkway running across the crest of the Blue Ridge

Mountains, she had been taught to run for the barn to get her pa and her brothers whenever a black man dared put a foot on their property. And Mr. Turner was one mountain of a black man—and as old as the hills in whose shadows she had grown up and whose embrace she had fought so hard to escape by coming down to Charlottesville for a job.

"Morning, Mr. Turner. Strong coffee with cream and sugar as always?"

"Thanks, Trixie. Yes, as strong as always. Nobody can make strong coffee like The Nook."

He said the same thing a good four days out of five. It meant he was in a good mood. That meant there would be a good tip this morning. But, it had been years now since Trixie had salivated after those great tips Mr. Turner dropped on her table. There was much more to Mr. Turner than his tips. They had become the best of friends, comfortable with each other without going to any special pains. She had to admit that to herself, although she certainly wasn't going to go up in the hollow and scream it at her pa's barn. Didn't even think she'd be able to admit it to Evan over at the sawmill on 250 west near the Crozet turnoff.

"Two eggs over easy with sugar ham and toast, as usual?"

"That's right. I've got to gather up the energy to limber up and do some practicing for this afternoon."

"You don' need no practicing, Mr. Turner. You're the greatest piano player there is already. Wish we had a piano player to play here in The Nook like you do in your restaurant. It would give us more class."

"Thanks, Trixie. The Nook's got atmosphere and history going for it. It doesn't need the likes of my piano playing. But thanks for the buildup. That's why I come in here every morning. You're the best picker-upper for an old man that could be."

"Oh, go on. You come in here for The Nook's strong coffee, and you know it."

"That's why I came in here for the first four years," Mr. Turner admitted, "but for the last three it's been because

I don't think I could have made it by Vera's passing without good, steady friends like you to meet up with every morning."

Trixie turned toward the window to the kitchen in embarrassment. Mr. Turner wasn't usually this forthcoming with his feelings. She felt flattered that he'd think she had helped him adjust to his wife's death, but she felt plenty tongue-tied whenever conversations got more than an inch below the surface. She took Mr. Turner's OJ from behind the counter and returned to the table, determined to lighten the conversation as best she could.

"Well, I've heard rumors that you have some new living arrangements now, and maybe you won't be coming around of mornings much anymore."

Mr. Turner put on a big smile. "Yep, I finally got Pearl to give me a 'why not?' and I feel like celebrating that this morning. I'll be gone for a couple of weeks or so come next month, that's for sure. Gonna have a little vacation—and not alone for a change. But I don't plan on any new living arrangements gettin' between me and my breakfast at The Nook."

"Aw, gee, Mr. Turner," Becky said as she swung by his table. "Trixie's going to be off the first part of May too, and she promised her best customer to me while she was gone. Now I won't have nothin' to look forward to in the mornings. Bad enough that Trixie's goin' off to get married."

"Married?" Mr. Turner exclaimed. "Why didn't you tell me about this yesterday, Trixie?"

"Well, I doubt Evan thought about it much before yesterday, either, Mr. T. He doesn't do a whole lot of thinking beforehand. But there's a tractor show down in Nelson County starting May 1st, and Evan decided that the best thing that could happen on this green earth was to get married and spend his honeymoon watching tractors pull things around the Nelson County fairgrounds. I've been trying to pull Evan in for more than a year now myself, so I guess this is my best shot."

"Congratulations to you—to you both. You can tell your Evan for me that he's getting the cream of the crop. The best of luck to you both."

"Thanks, Mr. T." But all of a sudden Trixie didn't look all that thankful. She abruptly sat down on—more like collapsed into—a chair at Mr. Turner's table, hunched over, and hid her face briefly with her hands. Mr. Turner let her be for a few seconds. In time she reappeared from behind her hands, reached into her pocket, and came up with a Virginia Slims cigarette. She looked longingly at the door out onto the Mall, but she stayed put. Mr. Turner knew that her craving for a cigarette always was a signal that Trixie was pretty wound up about something. She didn't do that much smoking that he knew of and usually didn't get near a cigarette while she was working.

"Whatsa matter, Trixie?" Mr. Turner finally asked. "Second thoughts about your young man?" The sad-eyed look she gave him made his heart wrench.

"Naw, thanks. Evan's the one for me. I don't have no complaints in that department."

"Then, what is it? I hate to see you sad, especially at a time that should be bringing you the most enjoyment. And for sure not on a day that I'm celebrating havin' someone to go home to again."

"Yeah, right. Weddings are supposed to be the highlight of a girl's life, ain't they? I guess I just always got tied up with the fantasies that every girl carries around about their weddings. Just because I was raised up in the hollows don't mean I didn't have the life of a fairy princess mapped out. Evan's the right Prince Charming—at least in looks and in having a good heart in the right place, and he's a hard worker—but I was no different from those girls in Farmington and Keswick. I wanted it to be storybook perfect. You know, frilly white dress, three-tiered cake, that wonderful little stone chapel on the Keswick road, a small orchestra, and three nights at the Greenbriar. So here it comes: my only good church dress, a justice of the peace in Crozet, five days at the Nelson County tractor pull, a rented bungalow on the side of the highway, and back to work for both of us."

"Your dream doesn't sound all that pushy to me," Mr. Turner said softly. "You know, Vera once admitted that she had had a fantasy about her wedding too. But we didn't even have a tractor pull to go to. I was down in New Orleans trying to make a go of it with stiff competition. Seems before we thought of having a honeymoon again, Vera no longer felt up to it. It seems pretty bad planning on the Almighty's part that when we're young enough to enjoy life, we don't have two nickels to rub together, and when we've reached a level of comfort, we're too busy to enjoy life and we just sit on useless bank accounts. Until one day life comes and strikes us down. It all seems so senseless, or maybe God's just a big joker."

"Now, don' let me get you down, Mr. Turner. You walked in here floatin' on air and I'll feel bad if you don' leave that way. Evan's a real hunk. I'm going to have a ball in that rented bungalow with my man. And you've got yourself Pearl now and a nice vacation for two planned as well. That's great. That's just what you need. You've pined away on your missus too long. I met her a couple of times, there toward the end, and she told me she wanted you to get more out of life than you had to that point."

"A couple of times?" Mr. Turner snorted. "You was over at that hospital more than I was. And you know what, I'm just as good as that orchestra you've been fantasizing. So, you got that part covered. I'll be happy to play the piano at your wedding."

"No, you're better than I ever imagined, Mr. T. I'll check out whether there's anything you can play on at or near the Crozet Baptist church's social hall, and you're on. But hold up. You can't play at my wedding. You're goin on vacation that week."

"The hell I am until we've gotten you married. You don't think I'd leave town and miss your wedding, do you? I'll just start my vacation after the festivities have wound down."

Trixie didn't know why this gave her such a lift, but it did. She briefly thought about her pa and her brothers, seeing Mr. T. show up at her wedding. But it was past time for them to join the real world, anyhow. She'd just give them a good talking to beforehand, and then they could just decide for themselves whether they would be there, 'cause she'd decided here and now that Mr. Turner would be there.

She bounced up and went for Mr. Turner's eggs. The morning got pretty busy along about then, and every time she thought of checking on her good customer, he looked pretty deep in thought. He also was doing some figuring with a pen on his napkin, as he often did when he was working on his business plans. Trixie hoped that he wasn't having second thoughts about his new living arrangements and his coming vacation—or about telling yet another woman that he was putting their plans off to take care of other business. She hadn't lied about Vera wanting him to get on with his life. They'd been such a nice couple. She decided she'd hate not having him at her wedding—a strange thought, it occurred to her, because up to fifteen minutes ago she had had no intention of inviting him to her wedding—but she couldn't see him putting off his vacation plans for her. She'd sit down and talk it over with him again before he finished his breakfast and left.

Next thing she knew, Mr. Turner had finished and was gone, and Becky was standing over his leavings with a very strange look on her face.

"Whatsa matter?" Trixie asked, as she ambled over. "Mr. Turner forget to leave a tip for the first time in his life?"

"Not exactly," Becky said in a small, distant voice.

Trixie moved Mr. Turner's plate and saw that he had left a check this morning rather than his usual cash. It was made out to her, it was in the amount of ten thousand, seven hundred, and fifty-seven dollars and twenty-nine cents, and it was marked "one breakfast and one storybook wedding." On the napkin he had left at the table, Mr. Turner had tallied out the estimated cost for a white lace wedding dress, rental of Grace Episcopal Church in Keswick, rental for the Crozet firehouse hall and a baby grand piano, a three-tiered cake from Chandlers, catered refreshments and champagne for eighty guests, four nights for two at a B&B in Nelson County, and three nights at the Greenbriar. The seven dollars and twenty-nine cents was tallied out as the cost of his breakfast.

The Present

I thought that what had caught my attention was how the teenage boy moved a few paces away from our front window and then stopped dead in his tracks and then, after a short pause, squared his shoulders and marched back to our window, where he stopped again only briefly before entering the store. But it wasn't his movement that made me notice him. It was his eyes, those sad eyes.

"Hey, look at that kid out front, Tina," I had said to the other sales girl in the Geldhaus when the boy had first stopped in front of our window. "We'd better keep an eye on that one. He's been looking at the stuff in the window for some time but not really looking at it, if you know what I mean. I keep telling Mr. G. he shouldn't put the good jewelry in the window. Someday one of those kids is going to put a brick through the window, grab some of that stuff, and be down the Downtown Mall and in the crowd before we can do anything about it. But look at him, so sad looking. Such sad eyes. Maybe he just needs to get something for his girl and realizes he can't afford anything in that window."

Tina put down the silver tray she had been polishing and started to come around the end of the counter.

"No. It's OK, he's going away," I told her. "Pay attention, kid," I said to the window, knowing he couldn't hear me. "You're going to knock over that old couple. Must be getting warmer; haven't seen that pair out on the Downtown Mall since last summer. Her always yapping away and him looking so sour. Boy, I hope I don't live to be that old and doubled up. Oh, but look. The kid stopped and turned around and is coming back. I guess he likes his girl too much to let his shyness win out."

The boy seemed to have found a new determination, because he came straight to the door, which set off that annoying bell when he opened it, and walked right up to the counter in front of me.

"Yes, sir, welcome to Geldhaus, finest jewelers in Charlottesville. Can I help you with anything? We have some nice school pins—both UVa and the area high schools."

"Um, no, I'm not looking for anything to buy. I was just wondering—"

He suddenly seemed at a loss for words and only half as brave and determined as he had been when he walked in. I didn't help. So far I didn't have a clue what he had come in to get, and Mr. G. always said not to assume too fast that the customer is looking for something cheaper than you might otherwise convince them they can't live without.

"Is this Mr. Gelton's shop? Mr. Gerhard Gelton?"

"Yes, it is. Did you want to talk with him? I think he might be in back, but he's working on a setting right now, and we don't like to disturb him when he's doing that."

All of a sudden the boy looked about ten years younger and ready to cry.

"But if it's important," I rushed on, "I can go get him." I don't think I could have stood it to see the boy cry. His sad eyes alone melted my heart. He was going to be a real killer with the girls in a year or two if he could keep that look.

"No, it's OK. Maybe you can help me. My mother said my father used to shop here—even before you moved to the Downtown Mall. And I think he knew Mr. Gelton pretty well." There was a pause, as the boy absentmindedly played in a tray of cheap stickpins on top of the counter. "Do you—?" He cleared his throat and looked up at one of the dim corners of the ceiling. "Do you perhaps keep any records of things ordered but never picked up?"

"I'm sorry, I don't follow. What do you mean?"

And then it all came out in a rush. "Well, I think my father may have bought something in here sometime before the second week in January and then not picked it up. I'm just checking on whether that could have happened. And, and, of course, I'd take it now and pay for it."

"Well, I don't know. That's possible, of course. What did he order?"

"I don't know."

"You don't know? This is getting a little complicated. I think I'd better go get Mr. Gelton. Tina," I said with a meaningful look. "Could you watch after the shop while I'm gone?" For all I knew this was just some scheme I'd never encountered before for a snatch and run. Tina moved ever so slightly between the boy and the front door while I went into the back.

Mr. Gelton was none too happy to be interrupted, the old grouch. Such a grump and miser. Never a kind word for anyone and wouldn't walk across the room to do a favor. I'd have found other work a long time ago if I didn't like his long-suffering wife, Milly, so much.

"Whadcha want? Can't you see I'm finishing up Milly's anniversary present?"

I couldn't help myself when I saw the exquisite diamond pavé heart pin. "It's gorgeous, Mr. G. She'll love it." I wasn't too sure about the last comment. Just the other day Milly had told me that she bet Mr. G. would give her another of those heaps of stones he makes for their anniversary, when she'd really settle on a kind word for someone from the old coot. Well, to each their own, I guess. I wished for the umpteenth time that I had married a jeweler—although I could certainly see her point about wishing that Mr. G. could be a lot nicer.

"This other one's very nice too," I said, picking up a diamond and ruby cross pin, with inferior but still very good stones. "Who are you making this for, Mr. G.?" I asked. "I don't remember an order for one of these. Such an interesting design."

"Don't know myself," he grumped back at me. "I just had this urge to make that one. Something just kept nagging at me that I could find a use for that. The arrangement of the stones just kept cropping up in my head. So I went ahead and made it. Now skedaddle so I can finish the heart before I forget which stone I was going to use to finish it off."

"I came to tell you there's a boy out front to see you, Mr. G. He says something about his father having had something made here and that it's on layaway, but he doesn't know what it is. I thought you might know what he's talking about."

"In a minute, in a minute."

I went back to the shop, and the boy, Tina, and I sort of wandered around nervously for several minutes, waiting for Mr. G. to finish the broach and put in an appearance.

Eventually, the curtains to the back swept aside and Mr. G. came in, muttering to himself something nasty about having been disturbed. Then he looked at the boy and said, "Don't I know you? Aren't you Pete Jones' kid?"

"Yes sir," the kid answered softly. "I'm Pete too, Pete Junior."

"Good man, Pete. We served together for many years in the Lion's Club. Sorry to hear about his passing. Met your mother too. Mary Elizabeth isn't it? Cancer wasn't it that got him? And it had a grip on him for quite some time, didn't it?"

"Yes, sir. Thank you, sir. Yes. The chemo seemed to have worked and then he had that heart attack and went so fast. Mary Catherine, sir. My mother's name is Mary Catherine."

"Ah, yes. Now I remember. Well, what can we do for you, son? Carol says you think your dad may have ordered something here and not picked it up."

"Yes, sir. Maybe he did and maybe he didn't. And maybe he ordered it somewhere else. The thing is, sir, it's my mother. She's so sure that he ordered a birthday present for her and never got to pick it up. It's not the present itself that's worried her—it's just the thought that his business isn't finished. That keeps eating at her, sir. Dad died just two days before her birthday in January. He had been going to chemo right up to New Year's and he still had managed to get her a Christmas gift. Both Mom and I had offered to take him out in early January so he could get her a birthday gift, but he'd just told us he didn't need to go out. I know he must have planned something. Mom gave me a list of the stores where she thought he did most of his shopping. I've already been to every one listed on the Downtown Mall. If he didn't order anything in here, there's just one left to check out at Barracks

Road and then I'll have to go back and tell Mom I couldn't solve the mystery."

"And you've been in other shops on the Downtown Mall and asked them this question?" Mr. G. asked.

"Yes, I'm sorry. It's sort of embarrassing—going in and asking to check with so little information to go on. But it's my mom, sir. They thought everything was getting better, and then he died right before her birthday. She's just been so depressed, and this has been eating away at her. I think it will help if I can just tell her that I checked and there's no present coming. It's been several months, and she still runs to the mailbox as if something might be there that was on back order or something. It's like something might turn up out of the blue when she wasn't prepared for it—that it would tear her up to run across it unexpectedly."

"Well, the order book is over here on the counter. We'll just check to see if—"

"I checked through the book while you were talking, Mr. G.," Tina said quietly. "I couldn't find—"

"We'll just take another good look," Mr. G. overrode her. "Hmm. I'm not sure. Maybe yes, maybe no. You say you had no idea what he might of been thinking of getting her?"

"No, sir. I think I did ask him once or twice, and he just smiled and said Mom was worth something really special this year—that he thought his illness had been harder on her than on him. But I don't know. With all those medical bills and expenses, maybe he just ordered her some flowers on the phone and the order got messed up. Mom loves flowers."

The boy was acting like he was at the end of a distressing school assignment and was just so happy that it was over that he didn't care what grade he got anymore. He was even inching toward the front door. I felt so bad for him that he had had to go into several stores on the Mall and give that little story. But at the same time, I wished my son were more like him.

"Just a minute. You stay right there," Mr. G. said. "There's an order form here that suggests there might be something in the back room." He swept into the back room before the boy could take another step toward the front door.

"Ah, yes, I found it," he said after having been gone what seemed like an eternity. "Your mother was right. Your dad did order her gift from here. If I'd been the one who took the order, I'm sure I would have remembered it. He always came here for his special gifts. We had been friends for a long time. He was a good man. Uh, I guess I said that before."

The boy hadn't said anything when Mr. G. returned, but his eyes had gotten really big. Then, with as much dismay as admiration, he said, "Oh, sir, it's so beautiful, and it looks so expensive. I'm sorry, but I'm afraid we don't have enough—"

"Yes, a really good man and always a great customer, your dad," Mr. G. broke in. "Most customers don't put more than 10 percent down when they order something special like this. But this order form says he paid the full amount when he ordered it. Don't find as good a customer as that anymore. I think your mother will like this. He ordered the design especially for her, you know. See that little engraving there on the back? Aren't those your mother's initials? M. C. J.?"

I had remained completely speechless from the moment Mr. G. had reappeared with the pin. When the delighted boy had left with the gift in one of our best boxes and with the fanciest wrapping we could find, Tina brushed back a tear and said, "Such a nice boy, wasn't he?"

"Mr. G—" I finally managed to stammer.

But Mr. G. cut me off. "Well, I said I knew I'd find a use for that other broach, didn't I? Don't fuss. Get back to work, both of you. There are customers to serve."

My eyes rotated around the room and then I stared out onto the Downtown Mall. There wasn't a customer in sight. "Mr. G.," I said a bit more loudly than necessary. "You said you were making the diamond and ruby cross for an unknown occasion. That I understand, and you did a wonderful thing here today—and to be honest I don't understand that too well. But you didn't give the boy the cross pin. You gave him the diamond heart you made for Milly. And it was engraved with Mrs. Jones' initials."

"I know, I don't understand that myself. Not the engraving part. I pride myself in my quick engraving work, although it's a good thing I had already checked with the kid about his mother's name. But I don't know why I gave him *that* pin, either. It's just that I got back there and saw those two pins together and thought of what I would want to do for a wife who had taken care of me through a fight with cancer, and then I just couldn't give him the second-best broach. What I said was the truth. Pete Jones had always been a good friend to me. Came to the hospital to see me that time I had the broken leg, and I didn't visit him while he was sick—not once. And that's one fine kid he's got. It's a good thing I made that other broach. I just don't know what I'm going to tell Milly. You won't tell her she's getting second best, will you?"

"No, *you* will, Mr. G.," I answered. "Tina and I will close up tonight. You go on home. Stop at the florists and get Milly some flowers you think Mrs. Jones would have enjoyed receiving, take Milly out to a nice dinner, give her that cross pin, and tell her what happened here today with the Jones boy. And I mean tell her everything. Trust me, it will be the anniversary present she always wanted from you."

Just Two More Years

Alberta Adams went over to the door and looked out on the Downtown Mall. No long line waiting to get into the Commonwealth Bookstore. She unlocked and opened the door and looked first west, down toward the Omni Hotel, and then east, up toward city hall and the amphitheater. Except for that poor young girl in the oversized motorized wheelchair, the area looked pretty deserted for such a lovely morning. She was glad she'd remembered to pick a few books out to send over to the medical apartments for the girl to read. Only a few more minutes to opening, and not a soul in sight who looked like they were waiting for last call. She sighed deeply, relocked the door, and retreated to the back of the store, where she would count the minutes until she could open for her last day.

The last day. All these years she had told herself that she'd do this for fifty years and then sell out to some young couple for enough money for her to be able to keep the upstairs apartment. But now both dreams had been shattered. A book chain had come to town and weakened her position enough that she had to close. She hadn't been able to find a buyer for the turnkey business offering. A bank had bought the building, and she was not only being evicted from the storefront as of tomorrow but also from her apartment upstairs as well. And two years short. She had always kept her eye on that fifty-year goal, which had sustained her through some bad times as well as some good, and she had only managed to eke out forty-eight. Just two more years. That was all she had counted on.

But it was only two years. Why should she feel so sad? Maybe because she hadn't really set any other goals for herself in life. She'd been content with spending nearly every day of the last forty-eight right here in the bookstore, living life vicariously through her patrons. Most of them had become friends, family almost. She had never thought of having a family of her own. For years, the elderly patrons who had come in to browse and visit were her parents and all of the little ones were her children. Thus, this had become a serious goal for her. She was going into the solitude and isolation of a retirement home without having achieved her only real goal in life. She knew nothing about the activities of the elderly: crocheting, bingo, and so forth. But then she thought back to one of her all-time-favorite books on the new lifestyle of seniors, gave a little chuckle, and added motorcycling, fencing, and spelunking to her list.

But all she knew about were books. She had no idea how she would fit in at Rosehaven. She felt defeated, a failure. Served her right. She'd been such a "know everything" all her life—and had wasted all of it without really venturing beyond the Downtown Mall. She had started here before there was a pedestrian mall; everything she had needed had been close at hand forty-eight years ago, and all of it was still close at hand on the Mall.

She went to the desk and looked at the inventory list of what she had left. Too much. It would drain even more of her savings to get it all moved out overnight. And the storage space she had rented didn't come cheaply either. Why had she insisted on sticking with her old-world arrangement with the book distributors and bought her books outright rather than take them on returnable consignment as the big chain that was putting her out of business did? Volume. That was it. She only was able to continue to get the hot new releases before the other bookstores in town by keeping to her old arrangement. Well, it was coming back to bite her in the bustle now.

She really did need to turn some profit out of the last of these books, or she couldn't swing the suite of rooms she had picked out at Rosehaven. She had thought that at least some of this stock would go today, especially since she had marked it for "pay what you can." She had been looking forward to at least getting good books into the hands of some folks who could not otherwise afford to indulge.

Oh, well, she thought. It won't be so bad. I did some figuring last night, and I'll still be able to afford that small room on the first floor, the one with the air-conditioning system under the window and where I'll share a bath with Clara. I do hope Clara is tidy.

The time had come. Alberta marched purposely to the front of the store, unlocked the door again, and switched the sign to "Open."

"Stand back, don't anyone get trampled," she announced to the empty space out on the Downtown Mall in front of the door. But the space hadn't really been empty. Just as Alberta turned around, a middle-aged man in a white shirt with an American flag logo on it passed by. Alberta recognized him as a waiter at the Hardware Store Restaurant up the street. He obviously had intended to just scurry by on his way to the restaurant, but Alberta's strange statement to the sparsely occupied Mall at this time of the morning had brought him up short.

As Alberta retreated into the store with an embarrassed giggle, the man entered and started to browse the shelves. Within minutes, he had made two selections and brought them to the desk.

Ah, the first sale of the day, Alberta thought. Somehow she had always been a little tense until she had made that first sale. And she had always kept a mental chart, like the thermometer design they use to keep track of church building fund-raising programs, that marked the level of what she could afford to eat and buy that day from the day's accumulated profits. Half way up the thermometer and she could have a slice of that peasant white bread from Our Daily Bread; if she hit the top of the thermometer, she could have a slice of Black Forest cake from Hot Cakes. For no reason she could figure out, as the man approached the desk, she was thinking: An extra tube of toothpaste for when Clara mistakenly takes mine.

"Ah, a book on the writings of Thomas Jefferson and the new edition of *Gray's Anatomy*. An intelligent, if eclectic choice."

"Yes, ma'am. I've needed to get my own copy of *Gray's* for some time. I'm glad I thought of it right after the new edition came out. Here's my Visa card."

"How much should I put on the card for the books?"

"Excuse me? Don't they have price tags on them?"

"Yes, but didn't you read the sign when you came in? I'm closing the shop and this is the last day, so we've got a 'pay what you can' sale going."

"But won't you take a loss if I pay less than the price marked on the book?"

"Well, yes, some—depending on how much less you pay—but the retail price does, of course, have some profit margin built in for expenses."

"Looks to me like you still have expenses. So, I'll pay the retail price. I didn't come to America to do less than my part."

"Thank you, that's nice of you. Where did you come from?"

"From Guatemala."

"Oh, I've always wanted to visit Central America—in person, that is—I've often visited there in my books."

"Yes, well, I'm very glad to be living here now, though. Thanks for the books. Good-bye."

The man had lived in Central America—in Guatemala. She'd always wanted to see Central America. All she had missed by living her life within the four brick walls of this building. But they had been good years, and there were all of those people she had watched grow in their horizons and helped discover the wonderful world of books. Charlottesville was a highly literary town, and Alberta had done more than her share of promoting literature here. She had kept a stock of really good books that the big chains, with their emphasis on high-volume sales from transitory best-seller thrillers, wouldn't bother with.

Over the years she had given prominent display to the books of any local author, no matter how new or inconspicuous. And she had helped many authors make the leap into the publishing world by sponsoring readings and writers' classes in the mezzanine space she kept for gatherings and for the readers who came in to explore rather than to buy. More than a handful of current internationally renowned authors had gotten their start on her mezzanine. And many children and young people grew up loving books because she had let them read deeply in whatever subjects took their interest in the comfortable armchairs she had scattered about the store rather than hassling them to "buy or git." She even had a back room, where she and some of her friends entertained as storybook characters at children's parties. She had thought she made quite a charming Little Bo Peep, until some little tyke who was much too smart for his britches asked if she wasn't really playing one of the sheep because she had grown so wrinkled.

Alberta had returned to the front of the store, where she saw Renata from the Raven Art Gallery down the Mall appearing for work. Renata had acquired her interest in art right in this bookstore as a girl whose ambitions far outstripped her family's ability to indulge in such luxuries as books. Similarly, Glenda, the manager of the swanky Hamilton's Restaurant, who had just appeared in the door of that establishment across the bricked Mall, had been guided by Alberta to the management books that had led to her landing that job.

At that moment, Glenda caught Alberta's eye and started across the Mall. She examined the half-empty display cases at the front and Alberta's sale sign with some consternation before she entered.

"What is this that is happening, Alberta? I've only been away on vacation for two weeks and have come back to find you selling out. Have I lost track of time? Didn't you always say you'd be here for exactly fifty years? It's only been about thirty hasn't it?"

"Oh, land, no child. It's been forty-eight. You can feel free to take those years off my age, but not off my time here on the Mall."

"But forty-eight isn't fifty. Why are you leaving? You aren't ill, are you?"

"No, of course not. Just a little tired. Tired of fighting progress. A bank wants to open here, and we all know the power of banks. What's that expression? 'Follow the money?' Well, I've always wound up at a bank when I've followed the money."

"But what will you do now? And is the bank letting you stay in your apartment upstairs?"

Alberta shook her head. "No, I'm moving over to Rosehaven."

"But you're too young to retire and leave us and go to a rest home. I grew up with you being here. God, this makes me feel old."

"That's fine with me, I can use the company, and you've always been good company."

"But, seriously, Alberta. Are you sure you're ready to give it up? And why Rosehaven? There are better homes here in town."

Alberta looked away so Glenda wouldn't see her eyes mist up. "There's really not all that much choice. I haven't saved enough to start over again. And if I don't sell much of this stock by closing time today, I'll be lucky to get into a home as good as Rosehaven."

Glenda looked around the store with sad eyes. "Our cook told me that folks think you were thinking of retiring because you were tired of working. And we all thought you were well fixed for retirement. Well, at least come on over to the restaurant for supper. I'll treat you to a closing party, even if it's just the two of us. And I promise, we'll only talk about the authors you like."

After Glenda left, Alberta was actually grateful to be alone for a while. She had had no idea closing down would be this hard on her tear ducts. She hoped that the rest of her customers for the day wouldn't want to reminisce about what once was and try to talk her out of what had to be.

But Alberta wasn't alone for long. Shortly after Glenda departed, Mrs. Elizabeth Potter-Hanson from out at Keswick Hill sailed into the shop. She gave a tight little smile to Alberta in passing and then started walking up and down the aisles of half-full bookshelves. Alberta could guess what section she was in by the tapping of her cane. It wasn't long before she had returned to the desk with an armful of children's books. Alberta started to say something to her, but Mrs. P-H had already turned and tapped back down an aisle. Soon she was back with another armload of teen novels.

"Regressing in our reading habits are we, Lizzie?" Alberta observed when it was evident that her longtime friend's hunt in the stacks had concluded.

"Nope. I soon expect to have some new life in my house, and I want to be prepared." While she was answering the question, Mrs. P-H had been writing out a check, which she ripped out of the checkbook with a flourish and tossed on the desk. "I trust you don't need to see several forms of ID."

"Not this time, dear. You haven't walked out of here without paying for your books since 1967—and that was because of the riot going on up the street a bit. But, but—"

Alberta had taken a look at the check and was having trouble forming her words. ". . . but I think you need to be more careful with your banking habits, Lizzie. This check is made out for eight hundred dollars. You got the decimal point in the wrong place."

"Sign on the door says 'pay what you can,' doesn't it?"

"Yes, but—"

"You've been pretty honest up to now, Bertie. This is no time to renege on advertising promises to the customers. The sign says 'pay what you can,' and, as you well know, I'm richer than Midas. These books are worth eight hundred dollars to me. So bag 'em, and button your lip. Glenda tells me she's throwing a dinner party for you tonight at Hamilton's, and I've invited myself. So I'll see you later."

And before Alberta could say a word, that ship had sailed. She was quickly replaced by Mrs. Henrietta Stowe-Byrd, who looked in the front window momentarily, entered the store, walked back to the desk, reverently placed a violin case in the corner by the cash register and out of harm's way, and strolled the aisles of shelving. To Alberta's estimation, she was looking at the empty shelves along the top of the bookcases rather than at the books.

When she returned to the desk, she said, "I see you have some of my books in the window, Bertie. Do you have any more copies here?"

"Why, yes. They go very well, but I had ordered enough to get me through the summer."

"Well, I can't stand to see them here in a closeout sale. I'll take all you've got. Total up the bill."

"I can't charge you for these, Henri. Why don't you just go ahead and take what's left for free? I've made a pile of money off your books over the years."

Mrs. S-B snorted in derision. "I've been insisting forever that none of my books have to go for less than retail. I don't plan to mess up that record now." Alberta gathered up all copies on hand of her friend's books, and, as she was totaling up the transaction with shaking hands, Mrs. S-B's attention had returned to the top of the half-empty bookcases once more.

"These are ten footers, aren't they, and solid oak?"

"Yes, they are. And they've aged wonderfully. I'm surprised they didn't sell. These are hard to come by. They'll be even harder to store until I can get rid of them."

"Don't I know that. I'll give you thirty thousand dollars for the lot."

Alberta's jaw dropped. "I don't think they're *that* precious. And what would you do with all of these bookshelves?"

"We are redoing the library out at Rivanna's Rest, and I haven't been able to find the bookcases I need. These will do nicely."

"But *this* many?"

"You've seen the library at Rivanna's Rest. I'm surprised you even asked about how many I need. Besides, I'd like to have some spares. As you said, bookcases like these are hard to come by. Oh," she said, as she picked up her violin case, "it's a pity you can't come over to the noon concert at Christ Episcopal. I have a feeling that will be a performance to remember. I'll tell you about it at Hamilton's this evening."

Alberta didn't mean to be impolite and not respond to Henrietta's comment on the concert, but she was in a daze until several minutes after Mrs. Stowe-Byrd had left. Not only was she getting top dollar for the bookcases, but she didn't need as much storage space now and wouldn't have the aggravation of getting rid of them. She already was reassessing her position at Rosehaven. She was no longer thinking in terms of that small first-floor room and shared bath. A nice-sized room with its own bath in the back on the second floor was also available.

"Alberta. Alberta. Are you all right?"

It was Renata from the Raven Gallery.

"Certainly," Alberta answered, her attention back on the business at hand. "Just thinking about how long Henri and I've known each other. We've had a lot of good times. Some knock-down-drag-out fights too, I must allow."

"I just came in to gather up all of your art books. We've decided that, since you are closing, we will start our own little section at the gallery on art books. Wholesale prices plus 10 percent OK?"

The door opened and another friendly face appeared.

"Hi, Renata."

"Hi, Laura Grace. What brings a competitor to the doors of the Commonwealth Bookstore?"

"Mr. Eads sent me over. Even though Read It Again Sam specializes in used classics and mysteries, we hate to see the type of books Alberta carries become unavailable in town. We'd like to take over whatever inventory she hasn't sold. Is that OK with you, Alberta? Good. Oh, and Renata, did Glenda tell you about the dinner for Alberta at Hamilton's tonight? Hope you can make it."

Alberta hadn't been open an hour yet, and she had unloaded it all. The second-floor back room at Rosehaven hadn't lasted long at all on her thermometer chart. Now she could take her original reservation for the two rooms and bath on the second-floor front.

"Ms. A, Ms. A, glad I caught you here. Mr. Turner and I both have favors to ask of you. Glenda just told me you were still open over here for another day." Louise, the waitress from the Moondance Café on the Central Place who had an insatiable taste for the Mahfouz novels, appeared in Alberta's vision. But she had to take a few minutes to catch her breath. Good thing for Alberta, because she was a little out of breath herself, and she hadn't stepped beyond her sales desk for some time.

"Mr. Turner is stuck with that small storefront building over by the plaza for another two years before the corporate tenants he landed want to take it over. I'd like to take the upstairs apartment to be near my work, but it's too big just for me. I hear you've lost your apartment lease here. Any chance you could come over and room with me? We've always had a great time talking about Egyptian literature, and I'd like to have the company, not to mention the help with rent. Oh, and before I forget, Mr. Turner wonders if you could relocate your bookstore over in that storefront. He'd be willing to renovate to suit, seeing as how he could promise a lease for just two more years."

"Oh, my," Alberta whispered. "I'm not sure how I will be able to tell her."

"Tell who what?" Louise, Renata, and Laura Grace asked almost in unison.

"Henri," Alberta answered. "She's going to have to make do with fewer of those bookcases now—but for just two more years. Oh, and I hope you don't mind if I don't move in for a month or so. I've decided I want to take a trip when I clean all of these books out. Central America. Maybe Guatemala."

Poison Pen

(Inspired by the biblical story of Jezebel and Naboth's vineyard)

"Another batch of mail, Sheriff? Anything crazier than usual today?"

"Another couple of anonymous letters about Lamont Hollings up at his vineyard. And one of them pretty crazy, yes. From Grace Tingley. Says we should check for him pumping a mixture of water and formaldehyde into his grapes to make them plump up. Same as she was writing last month."

"She thinks he injects them one by one?"

"Apparently."

"Now that *is* crazy." Jake, the sheriff's deputy, gave a snort at the image of hunched-over Lamont Hollings moving down his row of vines and sticking a needle in each grape.

"That's Grace Tingley for you."

"But you said the letters were anonymous. How do you know that one's from Mrs. Tingley?"

"She uses purple ink . . . and monogrammed stationery. We get shit like this from her every couple of weeks. She's always razzing on someone. And she seems to have a thing about Lamont. Scared shitless about black men, I think."

"So Lamont Hollings is off the hook then."

"Unfortunately not. There are two more letters about him here. Ones we can't just ignore. One says he's got a still going up there and the other says he's got marijuana plants. Things we have to investigate. Ignoring them is likely to come up at election time—although I'm not sure but what ignoring them would get us the most votes. If he was doing that, there'd be folks hereabouts buying it and not being happy if they couldn't get it."

"Ah, not so crazy. Little hard to think of Lamont doing that, though," Jake said. "He's always been a straight shooter, even if he is . . . you know . . . and keeps to himself. And as crippled up as he is now, it's a wonder he can keep just the vineyard going, let alone any side business. Seems he'd be living higher on the hog if he had secret income. But as much problem as we have with moonshine and M.J. around here . . ."

"Yep. Can't just ignore it," The sheriff said. "And there could be something to it. People start suggesting things like this about a person. Well, where there's smoke there's often fire, you know. Works out that way a lot. Can't afford to just ignore it."

* * * *

Beau Jackson was the king of the hill in Racine County. He was FFV—First Families of Virginia—and his was the largest spread at the expensive end of the county. The head of his family had been the best friend of every banker within a hundred miles back seven generations. In fact, more often than not, whatever Jackson patriarch there was at the time was *the* banker in Racine County. Just like his father before him, Beau was ground zero at the local political party picnic, the one who was the center of guffaws, the boisterous jokes, and the lifting of the beer cans—and the one they always called on to start the trip down the fried catfish line. At the county fair, he was always the one asked to judge the pie contest and the one to pin the blue ribbon on the prize bull amid good-natured jabs and jibes. For all of this, all he had to do was show up and be Beau Jackson of the Racine County Jacksons. God surely counted him among his chosen.

Everything a man could ever want in life Beau Jackson had found in his bassinette that first day he'd been brought home from the hospital.

Beau's porcelain-blonde third wife, Jessica, twenty years his junior, was someone you could call "studiously showy." She was the sort of woman who would have been breezily termed a trophy wife in one of those big cities up north, or would even evoke knowing looks in the genteel state university town just over the Blue Ridge Mountains and up the road a bit. She was a woman whose smile and fashion-model face the photographers insisted on getting into the lens frame at any charity event. but no one could quite remember what she'd done to help make the charity event happen. Looking back on the event planning, the color themes and raffle prizes always seemed to be those of Jessica's choice, although she would not have attended a single planning meeting.

No doubt she would have been the perfect politician's wife—if Beau had had the ambition to be a politician.

Jessica's devotion to Beau was the most real aspect of her life. You could see that he was her whole world by the way she lit up and hung on his every word and movement. Just seeing that was enough to dispel those misty rumors floating among the young toughs down at the Pit Stop Bar about what a flirt she could be when she appeared there the few nights Beau was out of town on business, especially when she wanted something. This was a possible aspect of Jessica that few others could see—or would believe, especially after the family lawyer, Emmet Shelton, had a little talk with the regular patrons of the Pit Stop.

In fact, Jessica was considered pretty much invisible outside of the spotlight encasing Beau. To most, she was just an adjunct of his—his quiet, chief admirer among legions of admirers, her eyes turned admiringly to his face in any photograph they both graced.

When there ever was a discussion of the talents of Junior League members of the county, the one skill besides supporting her husband that Jessica possessed that all women could agree on was that her penmanship was exemplary. After reaching this conclusion, the women could look a bit confused, though, assuming that there should be more to say about the woman and somewhat surprised that there wasn't.

The Jacksons lived in the ancestral family plantation house in the shadow of the Blue Ridge. Jessica had had it redecorated in frigid white and icy blue and not a pillow had been adjusted in the parlor that guests passed by en route to the morning room at the back of the house, but had never

116

entered since the house was featured in *Virginia Living* four years earlier.

There were, of course, no third-marriage Jackson children, and would not be any. Beau was all the child Jessica could manage—or ever could want.

Although of much the same age as Beau, Beau and Jessica's upslope neighbor, Lamont Hollings, owner of the Hollings Hill vineyard and most definitely the last of his line, was anything but like Beau. His family had been in the county as long as Beau's had, but for most of the many generations the two families had existed in the community, Lamont's family had been owned by Beau's. It was only after the failed rebellion that the Hollingses had been given the rocky plot of land farthest up the side of the mountain in exchange for working on the Jacksons' place for another generation. Lamont was not invited to the political party picnics and was not, for that matter, exactly welcome at the county fairs. He wasn't disliked in the community as much as he was discounted and just blended into the scenery. He didn't work any part of Beau's land now. But Beau still kept in touch with Lamont, because Lamont had the one thing that Beau didn't have and that Beau wanted.

Lamont had a vineyard that produced the sweetest grapes in the county.

Mother Nature is certainly capricious. Lamont had a couple of acres of land on his slope that raised the choicest and plumpest grapes, of the prime varieties that were coveted by all of the fancy vineyards popping up all over the county to attract the wine-loving tourists. Beau wanted to grow such luscious grapes himself, and he wanted to open his own winery to celebrate them. But even though he put in vines that extended right up to his boundary with Lamont's abundant vineyard, each year Lamont's plump grapes were contrasted by Beau's shriveled raisins.

At least once a month Beau got into his Jaguar and raised dust all the way up to Lamont's shack to offer him a yet-sweeter deal, in Beau's mind, for his vineyard. And every time he did so, his Jaguar came skittering back down the dirt road in failure, with its dejected tailpipe between its wheels.

117

Beau was almost beside himself with frustration. This pursuit to have his own prize-winning winery was the most ambitious undertaking Beau had pursued since he tried to win a writing award in high school for an essay his mother had written for him.

He knew Lamont was getting too crippled with rheumatism to be raising grapes, and he also knew that Lamont desperately needed money. His own chats with his banker friends had made sure Lamont was under that sort of pressure.

Beau and Lamont were from two totally different worlds. The only one who was even speaking to both of them was Emmet Shelton down at the county seat, whose family had been lawyers and advisers to both the Jacksons and Hollingses for generations. As long as there had been a Jackson smiling benignly out in front of any ribbon-cutting line of county leaders and benefactors, there had been a Shelton in the shadows, making sure that the Jackson was the one standing in the best light. But the Sheltons weren't FFV. They had arrived in Racine County from Yorkshire, England, in the late seventeenth century, even ahead of the Jacksons. But rather than being the second sons of nobility, they arrived as indentured servants. From time to time a Shelton was known to remark that they were still indentured servants to the Jacksons.

When the Hollingses were emancipated, it was the Sheltons who set up a new, mutually beneficial relationship and maintained a peace between them and the Jacksons. Thus the Sheltons maintained as much cachet with one family as with the other. For this reason, Beau had tried to get Emmet to talk Lamont into parting with his vineyard. But Emmet had just smiled his fatherly smile and said he thought Beau had enough toys already and that Lamont probably deserved the comfort of a good grape harvest in the life he endured.

Lamont had, in fact, once thought of selling to the Jacksons and retiring to Florida. Rheumatism had set in and working the vines was becoming increasingly onerous without another Hollings to pass it on to. But when rumors spread about some possible illegal and unhealthy farming

118

techniques being the reason the Hollings grapes were superior, Beau's offer for the land had gone below what Lamont needed to retire.

The last time Beau slid down the hillside in his despondent Jaguar and stormed into the house, Jessica thought he might do harm to himself in frustration with Lamont's continued refusal to sell the vineyard. After he cooled down enough for her to approach him, Jessica took Lamont's hand, led him out to the screened porch, pushed him into a wicker chair beside a frosted beer, and began to massage his temples.

"There, there, honey," she said. "You'll get your vineyard. You know it will all work out. It always works out for you."

Beau opened his eyes, and the adoration and calm trust that were reflected in Jessica's face nearly took his breath away. Ah, the simple confidence of the young and beautiful, he thought.

"You're my rock, sweetheart," he said. "I don't know how you do it, but you always have such confidence and it always works out as you say it will."

There, indeed, was some spark in Jessica's eyes that bolstered his own confidence. Then he focused beyond Jessica's face, out beyond the screened porch and up the hillside, where he could clearly tell where his puny, withering vines left off and the gigantic, glossy-green leaves of Lamont's vines started, winding boisterously along their wires and reaching across the rows in splendid profusion.

"Shit," he exclaimed as he jumped out of his chair, turned over the table under his beer glass, and slammed out of the house.

Jessica looked up, startled, at the sound of his petulance. But when he was gone, she sighed; smiled a brave, but concerned smile; brushed a single stray strand of silky-blonde hair in place; and retired to her writing desk.

It was shortly after that that people began to notice Lamont in a negative way rather than just as someone up at the Hollings vineyard, someone who had been part of the wallpaper of the town for as long as anyone else had been

119

there. This wasn't because of anything Lamont was doing—that they could see—but because of what the letters implied. At first most people just laughed the letters off, not being able to imagine that Lamont was capable of doing, let alone prone to be doing, what the letters said about him. But then the stories began to circulate down at the Pit Stop Bar, where they acquired depth and dimension. After they had floated through Reid's Grocery and the Baptist Women's Reading Club, at least bits and pieces of what was being said began to sink in and to be given some credence.

By the evening when Beau was in Richmond and Jessica Jackson stumbled, disheveled, into the Pit Stop Bar and mumbled through swollen lips to the regulars Fred Singleton and Wayne Bob Wilson that she had been assaulted by Lamont Hollings out in the parking lot, the stories about Lamont were no longer being discounted as ridiculous in the community. Fred and Wayne Bob strode out of the bar and up the hillside to where Lamont was standing by his vineyard and sluicing the sweat of a day's work off himself as best he could with his crippled hands—and they beat him senseless. According to a front-page article three days later in the *Racine County Register*, a reportedly remorseful Lamont swallowed the barrel of a hunting rifle and pulled the trigger.

Half the county attended the auction of the Hollings land, although no one other than Beau would have even thought about bidding for the vineyard parcel. A glad-handing Beau was there, of course, a fact that an enraged Emmet Shelton was quick to throw back into his face.

"How could you be any part of this, Beau?" Emmet asked, his face as sorrowful as anyone had ever seen.

"Excuse me?" Beau responded in confusion with an edge of hurt. "I did nothing. I did nothing at all. I'm not guilty of anything."

"Of course you did nothing, Beau. You've done nothing all of your life. You've never had to do anything. There's always been someone there to do it for you. I don't know who did this for you, but this isn't just about you now. Half the county will assume that I did this. That's what the

Sheltons have done for the Jacksons forever—finagled for you whatever you coveted."

"It's just fate; it's just all worked out for the best," Beau persisted. "There are no more Hollingses. The land is being auctioned; there's no reason why I shouldn't bid on it. I didn't do anything."

"No, I believe you didn't do this. But you know what was done. And you are here getting the land you wanted—and that everyone knew you wanted—aren't you?"

Beau just stood and stared at Emmet. It wasn't a mean stare; it was a bewildered stare, a stare that was totally devoid of any flicker of understanding. Jessica, clinging to Beau's side, was the one showing the belligerent, defending-her-man stare—and the understanding.

And as the other members of the community became aware of Beau and Emmet facing off at each other, they wavered only momentarily before almost imperceptibly shrinking away from Emmet and into a protecting circle around Beau and Jessica.

* * * *

Emmet learned of the new set of letters circulating two weeks later, letters that told lies about *him*. A week after that he moved to that genteel state university town just over the Blue Ridge mountains and up the road a bit. But he continued subscribing to the *Racine County Register* and couldn't help but give a small, grim smile the day, not too many months later, when he opened the paper and saw the report that a sudden blight had destroyed all of grapevines on Racine County's Blue Ridge Mountain slopes.

If there was one thing that Racine County was known for, it was the grip that fundamental religion had on it. Fundamentalism permeated the atmosphere there to the extent that the *Racine County Register* article on the blight quoted several local ministers as blaming the natural disaster on what had become the county's leading money crop on licentious, un-Christian living. There even were references to the cursed, poisoned biblical era of Jezebel and Ahab.

These references stuck in Emmet's mind all through the evening until he was sitting in the darkness and reviewing not just his own life but the whole social structure of Racine County as well. Late that evening, having struggled with his own demons, he gave a dry little laugh, hauled his bulk out of his wing chair, went to his writing desk, turned on a light, searched and found his address book, and reached for pen and letter paper.

A Place at the Table

(Inspired by the biblical story of Jacob and Esau and the parable of the prodigal son)

The two brothers could not have been more different—and this quite possibly had something to do with their incessant bickering when they were younger and their more serious fighting when they had gotten older. John and Jim were only about twelve months apart, but from the time they were very young, John, the older, had been solid as a rock. Even before he'd learned to talk, he had been at his dad's elbow in the auto repair garage at the rural crossroads near Port Republic, in the western shadow of the Blue Ridge Mountains, handing his dad wrenches and trying to get his nose into the engine compartment to see what his father was working on. He wasn't all that bright in school and was very shy around people. But he sure did know how to fix a car and please a customer—and to make his dad proud. Jim was another story altogether. Smart as a whip and a whiz at the wise cracks, he was always surrounded by friends but also was always viewed a little suspiciously by adults, who unconsciously held onto their wallets or purses whenever Jim and his crowd had been around. If there was a community sports event, spelling bee, or some sort of contest of intelligence, though, Jim was always the winner of his class. And in this, he always made his dad proud.

Dad was equally proud of his sons, but Mom was quite different. She was a city girl and pined away at the rural crossroads. Joe's steadiness and contentment seemed to grate on her, and she saw a matching soul in her Jim. She could tell by the blaze in his eyes and his innate intelligence that he not only was capable of great things, but also that this country outpost was not going to hold him. In those final months in which she was wasting away and Dad threw himself wholly into the work at the garage to avoid the truth of what was happening, it was Joe who did the cooking and cleaning and

123

fetching to her bed. But she only had eyes for Jim, who sat beside her, patting her hand and weaving stories of far-off kingdoms and golden grails to help ease her terror of the truth.

Although the younger, Jim always was miles ahead of Joe in getting what he wanted. As youngsters sent in to clean their shared room, they'd both get a start, but it would only be minutes until Jim went into action.

"I gotta go to the can, Joe. Be right back. But, boy, this is man's work, and it looks like I'm the only one who can do this right."

And when he returned, about an hour later, "Umm, sorry, the phone rang before I could get back. But, oh, look. The room's already done. You're the man, Joe."

And Joe would beam with pleasure that he'd done what Jim thought only *he* could do.

But Joe wasn't so dim that he didn't eventually catch on to his brother's tricks. Pretty soon he began to resent Jim's approach to life and his ability to wind his doting parents around his finger. But he didn't resent it enough to change his own steady nature.

The boys were in their teens when their mother died, and that pretty much opened the floodgates on their mutual hostility and the tension around the compound. Joe continued to take charge in the house and also had to work harder in the garage, because his father couldn't seem to fully snap out of the loss of his mother. Jim got a job at the movie theater in a town twenty miles away and acquired an expensive girlfriend—so, of course Dad had to buy him a flashy convertible to get to work in.

Then came the day when an old movie house in Staunton was up for sale and Jim and a couple of his friends decided they wanted to buy it. Their plans were to expand into the storefront at one side with a pool hall; a bar; and, although Jim's dad was never informed, a room for poker and betting in the back. Jim's partners-to-be had their share of the necessary front money. Jim, of course, did not. But Jim was the brains of the venture and its big-smile front man.

"I've talked it over with Dad," Jim said. He had waited until the evening, when Joe had sat down to the account books. "He agrees that I can take my third out of the farm and garage now and go into business for myself over in Staunton."

"Your third? Dad agreed that his garage includes a 'your third,' does he? This business that only Dad and I have worked to maintain."

"Dad said you'd write a check," Jim shot back. "That since he sold the lower forty to that developer, there should be enough in the bank to cover a third of our worth. He said you wouldn't give me any trouble."

"Oh, yes," Joe responded after a long pause. "He did talk to me about it. He said family was family and that Mom had begged him before she died to let you leave here when you wanted to. No, I won't give you any trouble. I've already written the check, so here it is. Take it and go." The delivery of Joe's last statement was as thick and cold as an ice cube; it was a miracle that he'd managed to get his tongue around it at all. Jim took the check and roared off in his convertible. He didn't need to pack; he'd moved into his girlfriend's apartment months earlier.

Joe was still cooking the meals, but in recent months Dad had worked his way up to leaving the garage early enough to get cleaned up and set the table. That evening, when Joe walked in from the kitchen, casserole in hand, he was surprised to see three places set at the table. Dad had been setting three places there for dinner even though Jim had already been more-or-less permanently living with his girlfriend in Staunton. But Jim was gone now. The fear suddenly crept into Joe that Dad's mind was going.

"Dad, you knew I wrote that check for Jim today. You saw him take off in the convertible of his, didn't you?"

"Yes." The answer sounded sad, but it didn't sound uncertain.

"You know there's little chance he's coming back, don't you?"

A long pause.

"I mean anytime soon. He's got his money, and his car, and his girl, and his wishes. You know he won't be eating dinner here anytime soon, don't you?"

"Maybe not. Maybe not soon," the old man answered. "But he's family, son, and there will always be a place for him at this table."

And, as far as the father was concerned, there always *was* a place set at the table for Jim. They didn't hear much about Jim for the next couple of years. And after the police raided the back room at the pool hall and the movie house burned down under suspicious circumstances, they heard nothing from Jim at all.

But every night when they went into dinner, there was an extra place setting at the table for Jim.

It was nearly six years later when Joe heard a honk of a horn and came out of the garage to see an UPS truck pulling away from the house. He walked over and saw a package on the porch. Receiving a package here, delivered by an UPS truck, was not a common occurrence, and Joe found himself scratching his head in wonder. Joe was just as perplexed after he had opened the package as he was before. It contained a set of crystal whiskey decanters in a slightly tarnished silver-plate holder. The only card he found in the wrappings had "Peace?" scrawled across it.

In the twilight of that evening, an ancient sedan, obviously on its last wheel rims, pulled up in front of the house, and Joe heard the front gate squeak from where he sat on the porch behind the tangle of wisteria. Joe saw the car out front first, and his immediate irritated reaction was to assume that this was a customer for the garage and that the owner had waited entirely too long to try to save that rattletrap. However, this thought was quickly replaced, as it always was, by calculations about what Joe might be able to do to fix it up. But then he saw—and recognized—his brother, Jim, coming up the walk, and his emotions started going to town. The whiskey decanters sprang to his mind, followed by the thought that he should have known what would happen next after receiving those. Joe's emotions didn't show on his countenance, though. He'd learned to stay calm and keep himself well in check, as was necessary to do with customers in an auto garage business.

"Hello, Joe," said Jim, warily, when he'd stopped on the walk below the steps into the house.

"Hello, Jim," Joe replied. Nothing was going on with Joe's face to give Jim any clues.

"Long time no see," Jim answered.

"That would be an understatement," Joe responded. Still no sign how this was going over with Joe.

A long pause after which Jim moved his gaze from side to side and said, "Where's Dad?"

"Dad died more than a year ago, Jim. If I'd had any idea where you were, I would have told you."

"Oh." Another long pause, and then an, "Oh, well," and Jim turned to walk back to his car.

He hadn't made it back to the gate, though, before the voice from the shadows of the porch quietly said, "You'd best come in."

Jim turned and trudged back up the path and up the stairs. Joe held the screen door open for him, and Jim entered the house. The lights were on in the dining room, but not in the hall or the living room, and Jim was drawn to the light.

"But what's this?" Jim said as he entered the dining room. "Oh. I guess I assumed . . . I didn't realize you'd gotten married."

"I haven't," Joe said. "There never has seemed to be the opportunity. The garage takes a lot of time, and . . . you know me and socializing."

"But," Jim continued. "There are two place settings."

"Yes," Joe, the steady brother answered. "After you left, there always were three, but after Dad died, I took it down to two. Like Dad said, we are a family, no matter what. Dad always said you'd be back. And Dad never led me wrong. Welcome home, Jim. For Dad . . . and from me."

A Question of Wisdom

(Inspired by the biblical story of the wisdom of Solomon)

When I came to, Clea was there with me on the front porch on my house on the outskirts of Elkton, in the shadow of the Blue Ridge Mountains, fannin' my face for all she was worth with my letter. I sat bolt upright and grabbed for the precious letter.

"Don't you go mussin' that letter, Miss Clea," I said.

"Land, Dorothy, you give me a fright. I saw you from out at the walk, you on your back on the porch, your legs splayed out like Raggedy Ann, an' your dress up over your nevermind. I thought you'd died and gone to heaven."

"Close enough, Miss Clea," I answered, "close enough. Here, give me that letter back."

"It's not time to be worryin' 'bout no scrap of paper, Miss Dorothy Dent," Clea Stallings muttered through pursed lips. "You just get on in this house and sit down over in that chair while I call an amb'lance."

"There's no need for that," I let her know in no uncertain terms. "I don't need no ambulance. I need the preacher."

"Well, I don't really think you're that far gone, woman. I think some quiet time in that chair while I see if you have the fixin's for tea, and then we'll just see about what you need."

"Oh, I don't think I need the preacher for last rites, sister. I'm just full of hallelujahs I've just gotta let out."

"Full of somethin', I agree," Clea said through clinched teeth, "but not nec'sarily shouts of joy. Anyone in your family have a stroke at your age?"

"Stop messin' with me, Miss Clea," I countered. "OK, OK, I'm sittin' in the chair. See. I've sat in the chair. Now give me that letter. I haven't had a stroke; I'm just fine. It's just that letter that gave me a start. It was just a faintin' spell. The heat today hasn't helped much, either."

"But . . ." Clea started to say. However, she stopped and just threw up her hands. "Well, OK. You sit there, and I'll go check your tea supply."

"No, Clea," I said. "You sit here a spell too. I'm just so sad and happy and mad that I just need to talk to someone about it. I've kept it inside me too long. I just don't know which way to go. But seein' as how you are here, you'll do. In fact, you'll do just fine. So, sit down and let me explain."

There for a second Clea looked like she was headed in three directions at once and just didn't know which foot to put out toward where first. Then she gave a sigh and a little wave of the letter in her hand and sat down.

"It's about this letter, ain't it?" she said, as she handed the paper and envelope to me. "Postmark is Harrisonburg. Who you know in Harrisonburg would be sendin' you a letter stead of just pickin' up the phone?"

"Yes, it is the letter, and I'll tell you 'bout it, but first we have to let out what's gone unspoken between us for the last twenty-five years."

Clea looked at me a bit perturbed. "And what's that, missy? I thought we'd pretty much talked over ever'thing either one of us had seen or done since high school."

"Not ever'thing, Clea. Not nearly ever'thing."

Clea's eyes showed she still didn't understand.

But I'd finally gotten around to it, so I gritted my teeth and dove in. "Don't you remember that time your mother told you not to go around with me anymore and you ignored her and we met secretly for years—that time right after I missed all that school?"

"Oh . . . that." Clea's voice was flat, but her face had reddened.

"I had a baby, Clea. I had a baby girl. You've been a good friend to me all these years. But we've never been able to talk 'bout it. I had a baby girl, and I wasn't married or anything. There, that's said. I don't see that that hurt either one of us. Do you?"

"N-o-o," Clea answered. "But I don't see what brought this on today. Is it 'bout this letter?"

"Yes, it is, and I'll read this letter to you. But I've got to talk a bit first. It's been scary these last twenty-five years. Things have happened that I couldn't explain—and didn't want to mention at all for fear they would just fall through—but now I want to talk 'bout it. I want to talk to someone 'bout it until it either happens or doesn't happen. Oh, I'm not makin' a lick of sense, am I?"

"Not really," Clea answered. But she sat back into her chair and gave me a reassuring look. "But you just go on and let it come out your own way and in your own time, hon. I'm listenin'."

"Thanks, Clea. You're the best. You always have been. We never talked 'bout the baby, but you always knew, didn't you? I'm sure your mother made it all very clear when she told you to stop goin' round with me."

Clea didn't deny the statement.

"But weren't you ever curious what happened to that baby?"

"Yes, of course. But you never brought it up, so I didn't either. I was just trying to keep you as a friend. And that wasn't always easy to do."

"I know, Clea—and I appreciated everything you did and was for me. I was just so beside myself in those days. I was angry at everyone and ever'thing. And I'm sure the drugs were part of it."

"Yes, I thought so too," Clea answered in a quiet voice, her eyes lowered to the tattered braided rug between the two overstuffed chairs. But then she perked up and raised her eyes to mine. "But you shook that. You were a real trooper and an inspiration to the rest of us who were givin' those drugs a try. You cleaned yourself up real fast."

"I had help, Clea. I had a lot of expensive help from people my folks could not afford. But that was all part of the mystery."

"What mystery?"

"I guess it's time to get to that part. I've just gotta decide where to start. It's just all so strange and mixed up."

We both sat there in silence in the dimming light for several minutes.

"OK. I guess I'll start with Cindy's birth. There really isn't much worth talkin' 'bout in my life before that. I was off at my grandma's near Harrisonburg for that near year you didn't see me. My baby girl was mighty beautiful. I wanted to keep her so bad. I bet you didn't know—no, there was no reason for any of you to have known—but I fought to keep that baby. And I would have kept her if it hadn't been for that mix-up at the hospital."

I stopped then, and I knew that Clea was bustin' to say or ask something, but I needed to get it all out, so I jumped right back in.

"There was a suspicion that the name bands on my Cindy and on another little baby girl born about the same time had gotten switched, and the other baby—there's not a doubt in my mind that it was the other baby—died before they could get that straightened out."

A sound came out of Clea, but I ignored it and forged ahead.

"Well, that other mother was older than me, and a whole lot richer than me—and she had a husband in tow. She kept screamin' that Cindy was her baby and all about how she was too old to have another baby. This last part alone was enough to tell me she knew Cindy was my baby and that hers had died. But that woman had connections and money and position, and she had lawyers and a judge in that hospital so fast that I didn't even have a chance to think what I was goin' to do. Next thing I knew was that the judge in Harrisonburg was sayin' he couldn't sort it all out and that maybe the best thing to do was to send the baby over to Social Services there in Harrisonburg until we could go to court. I wasn't no dummy even then, even with all those bad choices and the drugs. I could tell where this was goin' between the likes of me and the likes of that woman—and I didn't want to see my baby over in the Social Services system for the months or years it would take for this to go through the courts. Because of what my daddy did to my momma, I'd come out of that system myself. That was why I was so messed up myself."

I must have been cryin' at this point and bunchin' myself up and trying to disappear into the chair cover design, because Clea got up, came over and sat on the chair arm, encircled me with her arms, and started patting me on the back. That felt good.

"There, there, Dot. You don't have to explain or justify anything to me."

"I know that, Clea. But it's time I explained and tried to justify this to myself. I haven't really had to do that all these years. That's what's so strange. Where was I? Oh, yes, I did what was sensible and what I knew was gonna happen anyway. I told that old judge that Cindy was my baby, there was gonna be no denying of that on my part, but that I could see I probably wasn't gonna to get her and I didn't want her goin' to Social Services, so that old Mrs. Landon could have her. The judge gave me the longest, deepest look before he—"

Clea sat bolt upright. "Mrs. Landon? Cindy. You're talkin' about Cynthia Landon. Of the Landons just up the block?"

I just nodded and continued. "That's right. My Cindy has been livin' right up the block from me for the last twenty-five years. It's been a real miracle—and a heartbreak at the same time. You know this isn't the neighborhood I came from. You were just as surprised as I was when I inherited this house with all the trimmings from somewhere mysterious right after high school—we always thought it somehow was Steve's people in remorse for him getting' me pregnant and then just walzin' off. But as far as I know, they weren't rich people either.

"For a while I had the fantasy that Mrs. Landon was behind it, but she never showed that much care for either me or Cindy. After high school, there was the paid-up drug rehab for me and there were the job offers, first at the nursery school where Cindy attended, then in the cafeteria of Cindy's elementary and high schools, and finally in the real estate office where Cindy worked right before she got married. The biggest miracle of all was how Cindy and I became close friends and how she's spent so much time over here because Mrs. Landon has all of those garden clubs and all that charity work to attend to. When Cindy got married, I was the one who was bridal coordinator. Mrs. Landon may have been sittin' in the family pew, but I was the one who sewed Cindy into her dress and who had the last word with her before she walked down that aisle."

It was getting along toward dark now, and I found myself tunin' into the front window, wonderin' if the front gate would creak and there'd be steps on the walk—or not. What bittersweet wonderings.

Clea broke the silence. "That's quite a story, quite a story to have locked up within you all these years. Both wonderful and tragic. It's all a little much for me. But why? Why now? Why did you faint on the porch, and what does this have to do with that letter?"

I sighed. I'd gone this far with it. Clea deserved to know the rest—to know what I'd only now learned myself.

"Did you read the obituaries in the paper yesterday?" I asked her.

"Yes, of course. You know I always read the 'bituaries," Clea snorted. "How many times have you heard me say Amen because my name wasn't listed there yet?"

"Judge Alexander over in Harrisonburg died."

"Why, yes he did. I did read that." A pause. "Judge Alexander. You don't mean he was the judge who—?"

"Yes, yes he was. He was the judge who gave my baby to Mrs. Landon. His lawyer sent over this letter to me today. A letter he said Judge Alexander gave him to give to me. The lawyer said there was a letter to take to Cindy at the same time."

There wasn't much else that needed to be done now beyond reading the letter to Clea.

"Miss Dorothy Dent," I read,

If only we had the wisdom at the beginning of our careers that we have at the end of them, we judges would be something to behold. I am writing you this letter, one among many I have had to write from my long years on the bench, to try to clear both of our minds of one great question mark, something I seem only able to do on my deathbed. I want to confess, although I was certainly aware at the time that you were not fooled for a minute, that I knew that the baby you gave up in the hospital all those years ago was rightfully yours.

I don't really know even after all these years of life and of work on the bench what the right thing to have done for that baby was. You were still a child yourself, on drugs, with no prospects for yourself, let alone for a baby. From a humanitarian standpoint, giving the baby to the Landons might have been the best for everyone involved, especially for the baby. Even you, at the time, seemed to know that it was best to give the baby up. But I do know that I didn't do my duty when I accepted your decision, knowing without a doubt, based on your willingness not to put the baby in jeopardy, that the baby really was yours. For, you see, I was paid for a favorable decision by the Landons. I took their money.

I beg your forgiveness for having done that. The only thing I can offer up to mitigate my guilt is to let you know, after all these years, where that money from the Landons went. It went to put you through a good drug rehabilitation program, so that you could be a mother to your baby if you ever regained custody; it went to that house on the same block as the Landon's and next to the playground where your baby would play. And when the money ran out, I did what I could to put you near your daughter in your jobs.

I cannot say whether I was wise or foolish to be a party in separating you from your baby in the first place. If judges learn one thing in their careers of being asked to play God, it's that they can't come anywhere close

134

to the wisdom of God. The complex problems of real life and the competing demands for justice just do not permit simple solutions. But if I can give you any comfort in the here and now, let me tell you that your decision to give your baby a better chance at life than you had, and your determination to take every opportunity that came your way to be part of your baby's life, show that you had more wisdom than the rest of us put together in the bad choices that faced us in that hospital.

As my attorney should have told you when delivering this, I also have sent a similar letter to—

The sounds I so wanted to hear crashed through my reading of the letter. The creak of the front gate; light, but quick, insistent footsteps on the walk. My baby was home.

Mothers' Lament

(Inspired by contemplating a meeting between the mothers of Jesus and Judas immediately following the crucifixion)

The robbery was a botch up from the very beginning and probably would have failed even if Chris hadn't walked into the gas station minimart just as the cashier had pulled off Jud's ski mask.

"OK, Pops, this is what happens to smart alecks like you," Jud shouted, as he shot the cashier in the arm at close range. In frustration, his next shot went into the video camera that was whirring away above and taking the whole scene in. He started to pull the ski mask back down over his face, but the next words he heard, from a very familiar voice, stopped him cold.

"Jud! What are you doing? What is . . . ?"

Jud pivoted around and leveled his sawed-off shotgun at the front door. Chris. What in the hell was the best friend he had in the world, his old school friend, Chris, doing shopping in a gas station mart at nearly midnight? He was a priest. Weren't they safely tucked in bed at this hour or saying their prayers or something? Jud wasn't thinking rationally, but everything was just moving too fast. He would have given anything to be able to rerun this movie and do something that didn't put his best friend in the doorway to the convenience store. What was this loud ringing in his head? An alarm. The video camera must have been attached to an alarm of some sort. And the wail of sirens started in the distance.

Chris just stood there with that big, pained question mark on his face, not wanting to believe what he was seeing.

Something moved in Jud's peripheral vision. A stack of boxes was falling. It was pure reflex action that caused him to swivel to his right and fire. A well-dressed man in a cashmere top coat was standing next to the tumble of cereal boxes, a deer-in-the-headlights expression on his face. At the bark of Jud's gun, the man fell over backward and pushed over a rack of potato chips as he went down.

As he watched the man fall, Jud saw that there was someone else cowering back in the corner on the floor of the store. It was a woman in a red coat. He started to raise the gun.

"Jud!" Chris sounded insistent. "Jud. Look at me." Jud turned back to Chris.

"Jud, just stop," Chris said in a level voice. He was past surprise now. There were people here who had been shot and who needed help as soon as possible. "Jud. Just put the gun down. No more."

Jud looked around him with the wild eyes of a caged animal. How was this all going to be put together again. Just a little money for the movies. That's all he had wanted. He'd just wanted to go to the midnight special at the movie theater. The sirens were getting louder.

Jud reached over the counter and grabbed a handful of bills from the open cash register and stuffed them in his pocket.

"Your car. We'll take your car," Jud said, as he pointed the gun at Chris and started walking toward him.

"Don't you think . . . ?"

"Shut up, Chris. Just shut up. Get in the car. You drive. I've gotta get out of here and think what comes next."

The priest backed out of the store as Jud bore down on him with his shotgun. Chris got into his car on the driver's seat, the barrel of Jud's gun shoved into his side. They sat there for several precious seconds.

"Well, let's git," Jud yelled.

"OK, just simmer down," Chris responded as calmly as he could manage under the circumstances. "Where, which direction?"

"Uh. Oh, left, up Jefferson, I guess. Now!"

Chris peeled out of the gas station lot and went west on Jefferson. Two police cars were approaching the store at high speed, and one of them separated off and followed Chris's car, in hot pursuit.

"OK, that's it," Chris said. "They have us."

"Not a chance, Chris. Take out across the river and to the interstate. We'll lose them there."

"Lose them there?" Chris exclaimed. "What we'll really do is get more people hurt or killed."

Jud jammed the shotgun into Chris's side and motioned for him to continue driving. Chris complied, but two more police cars were bearing down toward them from the west as they approached the bridge. Jud stuck the shotgun out the window and fired at the nearest police cruiser. To spoil his shot, Chris veered to the right. But he either had made a decision of his own or he overcompensated, and rather than going up onto the river bridge, Chris's car went down the embankment to the right and into the river.

* * * *

Hurry, hurry. Slow, slow. When they first called, Madeleine had quickly gotten dressed, although it seemed like nothing would work for her. She couldn't seem to get her blouse to button, and then she couldn't find her purse, and then her car keys just wouldn't materialize from her purse. The delay was probably just as well, because she had no idea how she would manage to drive herself from home to the hospital. Her daughter, Eadie, showed up just as Madeleine found the keys. Before they could leave, however, the telephone rang again, and now there was no reason to hurry at all.

Now everything seemed to turn to slow motion. And not just from this point. Madeleine sat at the desk next to the still-open door, and all she could think of was Chris' ear-to-ear grin on his seventh birthday, when they had gotten him that remote-controlled model race car. He didn't even wait to open his other presents. He was out the door and headed down the street for Jud's house, and she watched from the porch as the two of them guided the car back up the street— and then down and up again until it got too dark for them to see where it was going. Everything was dark now. Her beautiful, wonderful, brave son. All of the life gone out of him. And all because he had needed a carton of orange juice late one night.

Why would a mother have to bury a child? Her Chris had been a saint; he'd even become a priest and was working among the poor. This was all because of Jud. She should have been able to see what Jud would become from the time he was a young child. She hadn't protected her Chris from the Juds of the world. They had been such friends. And Jud, and his evil ways, had taken her Chris away. Oh, why did a mother have to survive a son?

Madeleine stood up from the chair next to the door, smoothed out her skirt, picked up her purse, and turned toward the door.

"Mother, what are you doing? Where are you going?" Eadie asked in confusion.

"We're going to the hospital."

"Oh, there's no reason for that now, Mother," Eadie said, choking back the tears of her own grief. "He's gone. There's nothing we can do at the hospital now. We must get you to bed now. You'll need your strength for tomorrow."

Tomorrow, Madeleine thought. It will be worse tomorrow, and the tomorrow after that, and the one after that.

"No," she said. "I have to go to the hospital tonight. Leah will be there. Jud's mother will be there."

"Oh, no, Mom," Eadie said, the despair of the situation spreading across her face. "This isn't the time for confronting Jud's mother."

But Madeleine was adamant, and Eadie couldn't sway her to stay home, so off to the hospital they went. Eadie had barely gotten the car parked, when Madeleine was off like a shot from a cannon. She marched into the ER and up to the desk and was already half way to the emergency surgical unit when Eadie pushed through the ER's glass entrance doors.

Madeleine saw the figure from far down the corridor. Leah. The mother of Jud. The man who was responsible for the death of Madeleine's beloved son. A woman who Madeleine had not spoken to since that first time Jud had gotten both boys into trouble with that high school prank. There she was, still recognizable as the Leah Madeleine once had known and had shared morning coffee and gossip with.

However, she looked diminished and very much alone where she was hunched over in the vinyl sofa. Two policemen were standing stiffly a bit farther down the corridor. They were obviously at a loss for what to do. Leah's heaving sobs were enough to tell Madeleine how Leah's own son had fared in the automobile wreck.

Squaring her shoulders and setting her sights front and center, Madeleine headed straight at Leah. Sensing her approach, Leah stood and turned toward her former friend. As Madeleine came close to Leah, Madeleine opened her arms wide, engulfing Leah, and the two woman sank back down onto the vinyl sofa in their shared lament.

Where's Karen?

(Adapted from a combination of various biblical references to "who is your neighbor?" and Isaiah answering the call in Isaiah 6:8)

I'm not sure when it first hit me that I'd seen her before. There is a flash of lightning at the bedroom window, and Sheba buries her furry little muff into my neck. She's tickling me with her whiskers, which is going to make it very hard for me to get to sleep. That and wondering where Karen is and if she's found someplace to keep dry. I can feel Sheba's heart racing; cats must be able to sense the change in air pressure. She must know that the lightning is just a forewarning of a strong thunderstorm headed our way. But maybe that's *my* heart that's racing. I turn to the other side and pull the covers up, but Sheba moves with me and digs in even deeper under my chin.

I'm going to have to stop thinking about Karen if I'm going to get any sleep tonight. Let's see. What has to be done at the office first thing in the morning? Another flash of lightning, echoed by a whimper from Sheba. I sure hope that Karen has found shelter. I wonder if she will have gone far from where I left her off this afternoon.

At one point I thought the first time I encountered Karen was when I was strolling down to the Charlottesville Downtown Mall on my way to having a coffee and reading the paper at an outdoor café. I turned the corner onto 2nd Street running to the Mall, and there she was, shuffling along behind a grocery cart filled with bits and pieces of this and that. It wasn't so much that she was dirty, but that she looked so like a rag muffin in those mismatched, out-of-season clothes and the straggly hair that hadn't seen a perm in I don't know how long. I wouldn't even have noticed her if she hadn't given me that shy, little smile. She was actually making eye contact. It wouldn't have happened at all if I'd had time to see her coming and avoided making eye contact with her.

How do I feel about that? What if I hadn't made that first eye contact? My trip to the café was ruined. She followed along behind me as I walked onto the Mall. I'd had to duck into the needle shop after I'd made that connection with Karen on the pretense that that was where I was headed in the first place, and then I couldn't very well have gone on to the café; she might still have been shuffling around out on the Mall. I don't know if I'd slipped and given a look of horror when we'd made eye contact—or if she'd seen me do it. But the embarrassment of being caught off guard like that . . . . It just made me *so* uncomfortable. We'd been talking about the homeless in Sunday School just the week before, and I'd been so self-assured about my attitudes about these people.

I close my eyes tight and try to clear my mind of all thoughts. This has just got to work.

I must have drifted off to sleep, because time seems to have passed before I am jolted awake by the thunder. The lightning again, but this time with ominous rolling thunder. Sheba is gone now. Who knows where? She must have found more security than I was providing her. I must have failed her somehow as her refuge. Yeah, I'm good at that. Now, I wonder what made me think of that? I turn over again, and then I sit straight up in bed and fluff the pillows.

No, that wasn't the first time. The first time was a few days before at Reid's grocery store. She was sitting on the bench near the front entrance with her shopping cart. That must have been where she got the shopping cart. I wonder whether people steal a lot of their carts and what the store does about that.

I flop back down on the bed in disgust and pull the covers over my head. Who the heck cares? Oh, why can't I get to sleep? There's *so* much I have to do tomorrow. And I'd promised to take Karen back to the free clinic for her results during my lunch—but only because I also was taking Mrs. Wilkins to check her blood again. I'm not sure how I managed to get myself roped into transporting Karen; working with Mrs. Wilkins should be enough.

Did I see any sort of shelter around where I left Karen off this afternoon? It's going to rain buckets tonight.

The TV news said a flood watch had been declared until tomorrow morning.

As if on cue, there's a strong gust of wind outside that sends the trees rustling, and the first big raindrops hit the window. A bright flash of lightning, a popping and sizzling sound, and the nightlight goes out. Oh, great, the clock alarm's going to be off. I reach over for the flashlight on my nightstand, and, of course, it falls into the narrow crevice between nightstand and wall. I fish it out, open the drawer, feel around for my travel alarm, and set it in the wavering light of the flashlight. I wonder if Karen has a flashlight in that grocery cart of hers. O-h-h, I moan, and flop back onto the bed and pull the covers up over my head. Shutting my eyes tight again and trying to purge my mind of all thoughts. It had worked before; it's going to have to work again.

Does Karen have anything waterproof to wear tonight?

"Oh, it's no use," I yell to the empty apartment. "OK, just bring it on." With that permission, the thoughts of Karen flood into my mind. What was she wearing on her feet when I last saw her. Would I have become involved at all if I hadn't substituted for Brenda at the church soup kitchen that day and Karen had actually spoken to me as I filled her plate, trying my best not to make eye contact, knowing then that I'd seen her before and unwillingly exchanged smiles. She talked to me; she talked directly to me. Would she have dared do that if I hadn't been surprised into making that first eye contact and being tricked into returning that first shy smile? What am I thinking? Why shouldn't she smile at me when we pass on the street and thank me when I've filled her dinner plate? What's wrong with me? We had been friends; why wouldn't she have the right to speak to me?

Another flash of lightning and the rain starts in earnest. I give up, flounce out of bed, and pad down the hall to the kitchen for a cup of coffee. I turn on the light in the kitchen and nothing happens. Naturally. The electricity's off, dummy. That means no coffee, either. Not even any coffee, I whine in my mind. I'm beginning to really feel sorry for myself. Well, guess what, there's no hot coffee for Karen, either. So, just stop your selfish whimpering.

I'd called her my friend in my thoughts. Now, why did I do that? Think.

* * * *

Yes, my friend. Well, more an acquaintance, really. But not just another stranger on the street. That was the real shock. And I'll bet Karen knew back there at Reid's Market when she smiled. She probably even knew it when she saw me avert my eyes and scoot by her at the grocery store. It didn't hit me until I saw her in the free clinic the other day when it was my turn to take old Mrs. Wilkins in for her blood test. Karen had been there, sitting patiently in the waiting room. We exchanged looks a couple of times while Mrs. Wilkins was back getting her blood drawn, and finally Karen voiced a tentative, "Brenda? You *are* Brenda Murray, aren't you?" And then it all flooded back to me. Of course this woman was familiar; we'd worked in the same office for nearly four months. This was Karen what's her name—Karen Jordon.

I must have been in shock, because I didn't respond immediately, upon which Karen seemed to shrink back into her chair. In that brief, awkward moment, it had all flooded back to me. We'd thought of Karen as the bad news girl. Everything seemed to go wrong around her in the office, and she seemed to be in a daze much of the time. Sometimes she reacted in strange ways, and sometimes she didn't respond at all. I know some of the rest of us thought she was a drinker. And then one day she just didn't show up at all. When I finally got up the courage to ask, I was told simply that they'd had to let her go. They didn't give a reason, and I didn't ask for a reason. I hadn't even cared enough to ask for a reason. And now, there she was, in the waiting room of the free clinic. And I was here too, trapped until Mrs. Wilkins came back from her blood test.

All of this must have flashed through my mind in less than a second—and I must have said something back to Karen, because the receptionist was coming over.

144

"Oh, do you know Karen?"

"Umm, yes," I responded quietly through a weak smile. "Yes, yes, we've met."

"Well, do you think you could take her back to Preston Avenue, toward the Downtown Mall, when you leave? She's been sitting here for some time and she's still too weak to walk that far."

What could I say? "Yes, certainly, I could do that." And that had led to future rides both ways, from and to that train track ravine behind the Preston Avenue Bodos Bagels, as they did test after test, trying to find out what problems Karen had that they actually could help solve. And as trip built on trip, I saw flashes of the old Karen I had known and couldn't, for the life of me, think why I had cared so little about why she was fired from our office and what had happened to her afterward.

* * * *

The rain isn't letting up a bit; if anything it has become stronger. But the lightning and thunder seem to have stopped, and just now, just as I am about to return to bed, the lights come back on.

All that I can think of is that cup of coffee; I need that cup of coffee. No, that's not the only thing I am thinking of. I'm thinking that I'm going to be having a nice, hot cup of coffee and Karen isn't. Where's Karen? Was where I left her on Prospect this afternoon near the creek? I can't remember. That creek always overflows in weather like this.

I fill the basket of the two-cup coffeemaker with grounds, and then I hear the meow. I turn around, and there's Sheba. I call her to me, and she just gives me a disgusted look and strolls back down the hall to who knows where? I don't know why, but that just makes all of the strength go out of my arm and I drop the coffeemaker basket on the kitchen counter and sink down on a kitchen stool. I'm close to tears. But then Sheba returns to the kitchen, walks over and weaves through my legs, and then plops down on her cushion in the corner of the room.

I shove the small coffeemaker to the back of the counter, open the cabinet, and drag out the twelve-cup coffeemaker and a thermos jug.

A half hour later, I'm pulling up in the deserted parking lot of the Prospect Avenue Bodos. There she is, over by that big tree, huddled behind a dripping grocery cart. Yeah, a great place to be in a thunderstorm; between a big tree and a metal shopping cart.

"Karen? Karen, I brought you some coffee."

"What? Who? Brenda, is that you?" She sits there, looking dumbly at my thermos of coffee. I look at the thermos as well. What a dumb idea. She's sitting there, soaked, and I've brought coffee.

"Yes, it's me. Come on get up. We're going home. The shopping cart should fit in the back of my van."

"What? I don't understand. Home?"

"I don't understand either, Karen, but we'll work it out. We'll work something out. Come on, you're getting soaked. I hope you like cats."

False Flight

Leaving the doctor's office, Fred paused for a moment to catch his breath and gather his thoughts. He couldn't say he was surprised. He'd thought for some time that it was no worse than a peptic ulcer—not that he'd been able to find the time and opportunity to do anything about that either. But when he'd vomited blood the other day and couldn't pretend any longer that there wasn't blood in his stool, he'd made the appointment.

Of course he'd brought Hannah with him. She never left his sight these days. Today she'd think the appointment was for her and that she'd had it. He wouldn't have to tell her today. He wished he never had to tell her. And perhaps he wouldn't ever tell her; chances were good she wouldn't absorb it even if he told her. The visit had been a long one, with the doctor going over the results of the battery of tests in detail. Most of that time Fred had been worrying about Hannah sitting out in the waiting room. But this was one of those days for her; she wouldn't have much of any concept of how long she had waited.

Stomach cancer. He hadn't asked the doctor how long he had to live. He'd asked him how long he'd be mobile and able to continue life as it was. It hadn't sounded long enough, not nearly long enough. He didn't tell the doctor about Hannah. He hadn't told much of anyone about Hannah—other than her own doctor, of course. So far he'd covered for her well enough, he thought, from their family and friends openly expressing suspicions. It helped that the two of them had outlived nearly all of their family and friends. They'd never had children. It eventually had been apparent that they couldn't have them, although they hadn't bothered to try to find out which of them couldn't manage it. They had each other; that had always been all that was important to them.

There wasn't anyone, not really, left to care all that much. And that was the problem. When he was gone, who would there be left to care for Hannah? She'd been so much looking forward to their sixtieth anniversary, two years hence. Nearly sixty years of marital bliss, something that precious few others could claim. How was he going to tell her that he wouldn't be here for that anniversary? Of course, mentally she wouldn't be here either—not unless cruel life had a reverse gear.

He put on a smile for her when he came out to the waiting room, and she smiled back. She stood up from the chair, a confused expression crossed her face, and she looked around for something. Fred stooped and picked up the handbag that rested up against the leg of the chair she'd been sitting in and tucked it under her arm. Hannah gave him a little smile.

"Was it a good appointment, dear?" she inquired.

"Yes, it was a very good appointment, Hannah, love."

"Was the doctor pleased that I had been maintaining my weight?"

"Yes, the doctor was very pleased with how you have been taking care of yourself."

"Can we go home now? I think Bootsie will want her dinner."

Bootsie, the cocker spaniel, had been dead for three years. "Yes, sweetheart, we'll go home and give Bootsie her dinner."

Who was there to care for her when he was gone?

He'd already checked out the home-care possibilities. They had lived in a small, but adequate house in a fifty-five and older community near Staunton, Virginia, for ten years already. But what care of that sort that existed there was prohibitively expensive, and everyone he talked to who seemed half competent told him he'd really left looking into that option too late. And that was just from looking at him and Hannah—not from knowing what he knew.

He hadn't needed the doctor to tell him it was stomach cancer—not really. When he had accepted it was something worse than just a peptic ulcer, he began checking into extended care facilities. All of them would separate Hannah from him. She would have to be in a separate unit.

They had slept in the same bed, eaten their meals together, been side by side for nearly sixty years. They might as well be dead if they were separated.

They might as well be dead.

In the wake of his death sentence visit to the doctor and the thought that they might as well be dead if they were separated—and if, within days of the separation, Hannah wouldn't even realize they had ever been together—Fred went to the computer and started checking into such organizations as Dignity in Dying and the Final Exit Network. He didn't really intend on pursuing that angle, but he was getting desperate—and oh so depressed. It was a heavy burden to carry, but he had no intention of asking Hannah to bear it. She *did* have good days. There were still days they could talk this out, but she was just too fragile, he thought, to share this burden.

He did some planning and arranged for the day and hour some nice ladies from the church they once had attended took Hannah to the beauty parlor to coincide with a time that there was a talk by some representatives of the Final Exit Network at the senior center. He went to the senior center and listened to the lecture. He picked up their brochures. It all sounded so final to him. It would be fine for him. It would be something he was prepared for under his own circumstances. It would avoid a lot of needless pain. But Hannah had always been so full of life, so optimistic about the future, even when she had been lucid enough often enough to acknowledge that the future was getting ever shorter.

He took the brochures home and hid them in the drawer where he hid everything he didn't want Hannah to see—the little presents he often gave her at surprising times and the bills for her doctor.

It all became something for him to think about tomorrow—not today.

Until the day Hannah signaled that it was today.

They were sitting on the small porch on the back of their cottage, watching birds skim across the surface of a small pond. It was one of Hannah's lucid days. His arm was around her and they were cuddling in a porch swing.

"It's OK, Fred," she whispered.

"Yes, it's very nice out here—more than OK; a really good day," Fred answered. He was savoring not only the warm day and the pond but also that Hannah was as much her old self today as she likely ever would be again. He'd taken pain medication and he was bordering on mellow himself.

"I mean that it's OK. I know."

"Know what, dear?" Fred asked. The foreboding was rising within him. She knew of his cancer?

"I know where I'm headed. It frightens me so, knowing that tomorrow I might not be in control, might not even remember you—us. It's a living death, and it frightens me much more than the thought of dead dead does."

"It frightens me too," Fred murmured.

"So it's OK, more than OK, with me. It's what I want before I'm just not here at all anymore."

"I don't understand," Fred said. But then he did understand. She had drawn the brochures out of her housecoat pocket, the material he'd brought home from the Final Exit Network talk.

"You found those?"

"Yes, dear. Did you really think you had a secret drawer in the house—after all these years we've been together?"

"I can explain that. It's not what you think." His mind raced. How was he going to explain the brochures? "I found them in the mail box a few days ago. I put them in the drawer before being able to throw them away without you seeing them. I didn't want you to think . . ."

"If it wasn't just me. If you were in this state too, this is exactly what I would like for us," she said. "Nothing frightens me more than being here but not being together as we've always been."

"Me too, Hannah. Me too." It was the perfect opportunity to tell her about his cancer. But of course he didn't.

What he did was to draw her closer to him and begin to reminisce. Every minute they had to reminisce together now was pure gold.

"Remember how we used to go up to the Skyline Drive on the Blue Ridge Mountains and hike?" she said as they were doing their remembering. "It used to be our favorite activity. Just the two of us. And of the special spots we found to sit and dream, as if we were the only two people in the world?"

"It hasn't been that . . ." He cut himself off. He'd taken Hannah up there just two weeks previously. But of course she hadn't remembered. This wasn't a day she should be reminded that she couldn't remember. "On second thought, you're right. We haven't done that for a while. Let's do that real soon."

And, in fact, a glimmer of something was forming in his mind. She did love the mountains. So did he. There was no reason why they shouldn't go up to the Skyline Drive and hike a bit.

She had let the Final Exit Network brochures fall to the porch swing cushion beside her. As Hannah closed her eyes, with a sigh, and snoozed, Fred picked up the brochures and managed to stuff them in his pocket.

* * * *

It was a beautiful day when they set out—at least it was when they started out. The temperature was warm, without being hot, and the sky was cloudless. There were warnings posted in the papers about hiking and picnicking up on the drive. It had been a particularly dry summer and fire warnings were out. That didn't bother Fred, though. He packed a picnic lunch—finger foods he knew Hannah loved—to put in his backpack. There were two thermoses each, one with sweet tea. Hannah was Southern through and through. It wasn't tea unless it was fresh brewed with sugar.

He had called for a cab to take them up to the drive, asking that they be taken to the Moorman River Overlook. That was where they had often started their hikes. There was a hiking trail, but they'd always liked to strike out on their own, relying on Fred's sense of direction, his handy-dandy pocket compass, and his training as an Explorer Boy Scout.

"No, just up to the outlook, please," he told the cab driver. "We have a friend picking us up. He just wasn't available to take us. And I don't drive."

That was just sort of true. He drove now as little as he had too. He certainly didn't feel up to driving up to the Skyline Drive. And that wouldn't have done anyway—not at all. If Hannah noticed that they were using a taxi rather than their own car, she didn't say anything. She was excited about the outing, but this was one of her "half here and half not" days.

She waved happily at the cab driver as he drove off and turned to Fred and said, "This is just like when you used to take me up to the Skyline Drive."

"Yes, just like that, dear," Fred answered. He was accustomed to days like this.

"Shall we hike along the road or down the mountainside into the trees?" She asked.

"I think today we'll go down the mountainside. Remember some of our special places we found down here, ones we liked to imagine that only the two of us had ever been to?"

"Yes, that sounds yummy," Hannah answered, as she started out walking along the road north, toward the Front Royal end of the parkway.

"We decided to walk down the mountainside, honey," Fred said, as he gently took her arm and started to descend into the trees at the edge of the lookout's parking apron. The view was spectacular to the east, down a fold in the mountains toward the Virginia Piedmont, laid out like a rolling blanket of green, scored off in white fences and smatterings of farm houses, many of them antebellum mansions, with formal gardens behind them.

Hannah was really too weak to be hiking anywhere. But so was Fred, for that matter. They moved at a snail's pace, but they had hiked all their lives, so they managed well enough.

They stopped every dozen yards or so while Hannah stooped to examine the same type of fall wild flower repeatedly, each time remarking how the last time she'd seen ones like this was when they went hiking in the Blue Ridge Mountains in the fall. Goldenrod, foxglove, gentian, beechdrops. She still could recognize and name them all. It was the sort of thing with this wasting disease of hers that always surprised Fred—that there were some parts of her mind that functioned as sharply as they ever had yet other parts were either fading away or completely gone. Would that he was a goldenrod flower, he mused, because he couldn't avoid being angry that he inhabited a part of her brain that was fading away. If he were a goldenrod, she would know him to the end. He was supremely patient with her, though. Occasionally he lifted a sleeve of his shirt to wipe tears out of his eyes. He didn't let her see this, of course. For her it was all smiles and gentle laughter.

The deeper they descended into the mountainside forest, the weaker Hannah was and the darker it grew. Fred only realized that storm clouds had rolled in from the west when he felt the first raindrops able to pierce through the lush tree canopy overhead brush against his cheek.

"I think it's raining," Hannah said. "Maybe we should go into the house."

"One of our special places is near," Fred answered, ignoring her apparent belief they were just in the backyard of their house—probably the house they'd left a decade ago to go into the retirement community. "We can reach that in a couple of minutes. Then we'll be dry."

"Remember this spot, dear?" he said as they came upon a large cylinder of metal resting in the underbrush under dense tree cover.

"Why this looks like the old plane wreck we used to hike to on the Skyline Drive," she answered, a tone of glee in her voice. She clearly was pleased they had come here, and Fred was happy he had thought about it. He didn't mind them being up here on the mountain, but he was leery of wild animals. The crashed fuselage of the small plane—here obviously for decades—was a protected spot. They had always liked to sit in the fuselage, eating a picnic lunch, and either pretending they were flying somewhere or spinning stories of how this plane wreck got here and if they were the only ones who had ever found it. Fred's scenarios tended toward the criminal—drug running and escaped criminals, whereas Hannah leaned toward medical emergencies and joyriding young people. It had been the weaving of these stories, with Hannah occasionally losing track of the scene she was spinning or just abruptly stopping and changing the topic that had first given Fred an inkling that he was losing her.

The rain was coming down harder, and it had grown so dark that the brief light from the flashes of lightning were in stark contrast to the gloom. The scene—the incongruity of a plane hulk here in the mountain forest—was eerie, and Fred could feel Hannah trembling in his embrace. He grasped her elbow and helped her over to the hatch door on the plane's fuselage that was half on and half off its hinges. They climbed inside, and Fred pulled the door to behind them.

Settling down where they had done so several times before, sitting in tattered cotton stuffing that had been pulled out of passenger seats, their backs against the curved metal of the fuselage, they cuddled and murmured of times past.

They ate the lunch Fred had brought and drank sweet tea from two of the thermoses as the storm raged outside their refuge. Hannah was obviously happy, her face all aglow, as she babbled about the wonderful life they had led, sometimes sounding completely lucid and at other times completely lost to him.

But Fred couldn't remember the last time Hannah had been so animated and happy. It almost was as if she knew . . . and approved.

Fred took strength from this. He hesitated as he took one of the other thermoses out of his backpack, his hand hovering over it when it was half in and half out of the backpack. But with a deep sigh, he took it out, unscrewed the lid, and handed it to Hannah.

"Here, dear, this is a special drink I bought for us . . . for both of us. But there are two thermoses. You can have all that's in this one."

"Thank you, honey. You're so kind to me. You have done so much for me. It's been good with us, hasn't it? I love you forever." It seemed to be a flash of lucidity. Just like she knew and was telling him that it was OK, that it was what she wanted too.

After she'd drunk deeply from the thermos, she laid her head on Fred's shoulder and drifted off. He hugged her tight, unable to keep the tears from flowing, listening to her breathing—until it stopped.

Then, with a sigh, he took the other thermos out of his backpack and a cigar as well. He loved cigars, but Hannah had never permitted him to smoke them in the house or the car. He lit it up, deciding that she wouldn't mind . . . just this one time.

The cigar half smoked, he opened the other thermos and drank to the dregs the liquid he had arranged to buy in secret through the Final Exit Network.

The end of the cigar was still glowing when he leaned his head against Hannah's and closed his eyes. The lit cigar dropped to the bone-dry scrapings of cotton batting they were sitting in.

The hot flames on the mountainside were visible from the valley below, hissing in response to the waning thunderstorm, but fighting for ascendance and spreading to the drought-dried brush under the thick tree coverage that prevented much of the wet fury of the storm from reaching the ground. The park authorities and the fire stations below were called and started preparing for a slog through the dense tree cover of the mountainside, assuming that the storm had brought a small private plane in for a crash.

But, though two charred bodies were found in the wreckage of the Beechcraft Baron, no flight plan had been filed for a plane missing over the Blue Ridge in this time frame and no one could figure out who the pilot and his female passenger had been.

The Last Word

"And, besides, the dress was blue. I distinctly remember that, because Dwayne told Hazel how well the dress went with her eyes."

Clem exhaled slowly, but his grip tightened on the steering wheel. He concentrated on the whiteness of his knuckles and briefly wondered how durable the plastic steering wheels were in these old Lincolns. It had been a very long week driving slowly south from New York to Roanoke via the Skyline Drive and Blue Ridge Parkway snaking across the rooftop of the Blue Ridge Mountain chain. And no one at the plant in Rochester could understand why he took so few family vacations.

"Hazel's eyes ain't blue. How do ya think she got the name Hazel? And who gives a shit what color the friggin dress was? We were talkin' about the new siding they had put on their house. But, anyways, I remember it; the dress was green."

Madge crinkled around on the vinyl seat and contemplated both this challenging impasse and the vast vista of the mountain folds down into the Shenandoah Valley on her side of the car playing tag with the views on the other side down into the Piedmont of Virginia, as the Continental floated down the Blue Ridge Parkway toward the warmer south.

Clem noticed, not for the first time in the last hundred plus excruciating miles, that Madge's gum was snapping and her triple hoop earrings were slapping against each other slightly off the beat to the twanging guitar music blasting from the radio—and he turned the volume up.

"No, it was a blue one, for sure."

"What? I can't hear you!" Clem smiled a grim smile.

Madge reached over and turned the radio sound down. The flash of devil red nail polish caught Clem's eye, and he fishtailed the Continental's rear onto the shoulder and came very close to bumping into the stone walls that had been built by the Civilian Conservation Corps back in the wake of the Great Crash of '29 when this road was built.

"I said it *was* the blue one. I was with her when she found it at the Goodwill. Most expensive dress in the shop." This said with a slight tone of awe mixed with envy.

"Oh, for Christ sake, Madge. You always friggin have to have the last friggin word, dontcha? Nothin' more important with you than gittin' the friggin last word, is there?"

A slight extra beat of time, offering the delicious tease of closure and yet giving full value to what followed.

"No, I don't. No, that's not so."

"I think it is. I think nothin' matters to you more than havin' the last word."

The subsequent moment of silence was drawn out enough that Clem started fiddling around on the dash trying to find what was loose and causing that irritating tick-tick noise.

"That's not right."

"What then? What's more important?" Clem exploded.

A few long minutes spent in screaming silence while passing by enough precipitous drop offs for Clem to ruminate on the ways of getting away with homicide and, barring the practicality of that up here on top of the world, contemplating the relative ease of suicide by car.

"Welllll. You could admit the dress was blue for starters. Because it was."

The volume on the radio suddenly went way up as Clem hissed out a lung full of air and counted to thirty. Twenty miles and just over a half hour went by of sulky silence with pavement so mesmerizing and curvy that Clem was getting seasick.

"You just missed it."

"Missed what? What in hell are ya talkin' about now?"

"The turnoff to Lynchburg. You just missed it. You promised we'd stop at the first mall we came to and there hasn't been one for miles and miles."

"Fancy not putting a shopping mall on the top of the Blue Ridge," Clem muttered. He, in fact, had picked the scenic, top-of-the-world route for this very reason. Madge would have wanted to stop at every shopping mall from New York down to southern Virginia. They'd never have gotten to Roanoke.

"You promised to stop the first chance we got today. You know I need some shampoo. And a gift for Molly. You know we can't show up at her place and stay a couple of days with no gift."

"We don't get to Roanoke until tomorrow, Madge. We'll be in Lynchburg in a bit. That wasn't the Lynchburg exit. We're lookin' for Route 501. There will be plenty of stores in Lynchburg . . . and I thought I told you to take the shampoo at the motel in Front Royal."

"It wasn't my brand."

"How do ya know what brand it was? And since when have you got a brand of shampoo?"

Silence for a long spell, and Clem was starting to settle back into his seat and a little smile crept along his face.

"For years and years. I've been using Prell for years and years."

Clem tensed up in the seat again and the little smile flipped off his face and onto Madge's.

Madge sat there, humming a tune. It was a different tune than the radio was playing. Clem reached over and turned the radio down, although his hand wavered en route, like that wasn't the tune he wanted to turn down.

"Besides, you took the motel shampoo anyway. It was gone when we left."

"Did not."

"It was . . ."

"Did not."

A turnoff materialized for Amherst and onward to Lynchburg. The Continental didn't even slow down.

"That was the exit for Lynchburg, Clem."

"There'll be another one," Clem answered. "That was Route 60. We're lookin' for 501."

"But there was an exit to Lynchburg right there."

"Why didn't you get the gift you needed in Front Royal? We were right next to a big strip mall?"

"Told you this morning we needed to find a mall. You know, one with a Bath and Body Works or a Bloomingdales."

"They don't have Bloomingdales in the South," Clem said, but he said it so uncertainly that Madge didn't miss the lack of conviction.

"How do you know that? When have you shopped in a Bloomingdales? Or any department store in the South for that matter?" Her tone was a victorious one. She knew she won a double with that.

A big chunk of minutes of silence until the Route 501 exit into Lynchburg loomed on the horizon.

"See, there *was* another exit."

"There was one back there too," Madge countered.

As Clem pulled off the parkway, headed down the mountain to the southeast, Madge dug into her purse and came up with lipstick and a comb. The vinyl seat cover sucked at her and crinkled in complaint as she sat up in the seat and readjusted the rearview mirror so she could do her touch-up in anticipation of being on display in downtown Lynchburg. She didn't often get the chance to be the best thing that happened in a town that day, and she didn't want to miss it.

"Well, I don't see no mall. What made 'cha think a town like Lynchburg had a mall anyway? There's been nothing at all to see since we passed by the turnoff to Amherst."

"Lynchburg is a lot bigger town than Amherst is, Madge. And, what's that over there? Looks like a mall to me."

"Strip mall, that's all."

"Well, a mall's a mall. It's just shampoo and a gift."

"No department stores in a strip mall, Clem. Least not in the South."

He suspected she was just guessing about that but also saw the danger of another endless-pit argument, so he just hunkered down behind the wheel and kept driving.

The Continental spurted forward for a quarter of a mile, past the strip mall, and into Lynchburg, with a loud rumble from the eight cylinders.

"Probably not another shopping center for miles," Madge said. "Miles and miles up the road," Madge repeated in a slightly mocking tone.

The Lincoln slowed down. Two more miles north in chilly silence that didn't match the heat waves coming off the pavement.

"There's something over there, Clem."

Three minutes later: "There was something back there, Clem. Looked like an entrance to a mall to me. It says River Ridge Mall."

"Christ almighty, woman! There ain't no mall out here." But the landboat stopped and spun around in a maneuver that woofed Madge back into her seat and sent her comb flying into the backseat. The Lincoln sped so quickly back to the entrance of Lynchburg's River Ridge Mall that the slight jolt and hesitation and slowdown, followed by the unrelieved pinging sound from the front end, left little doubt that something was badly amiss in the engine compartment.

"See, I told you. There's a mall here."

"Harumf."

"Pull on over there, Clem, by the door."

"That's a handicapped spot, Madge."

"Yeah, and we can park there."

"I thought I'd just go in myself. Fast in and fast out. I know what Molly wants. Russell Stover's candy. They got a Hallmark store here and we're in business. That's what Molly always likes."

"Not always. I'd like to get out of the car a while too, Clem."

"It's such a bother and all."

"I'd like to pick the gift myself."

"Oh, for Christ's sake."

"There, there's a good spot. Right over there."

"Right over where?"

"There."

Clem swiveled his head to stare down the line of tanned skin, bangle bracelets, gaudy rings, and devil red claws that directed his view across cracked asphalt and ended in an empty handicapped spot, right in front of the door to the mall. He huffed, but he pulled into the spot.

Heads swiveled as Clem pushed Madge's wheelchair into the mall. Madge was an arresting sight in her purple sweat shirt over a crinkling yellow skirt on top of chartreuse stretch pants. She was talking none too quiet and lickety-split, so she was hard to miss. Well worth the trip to the mall, this sort of sightseeing being what had drawn many to the mall today.

"Aw, would you look at those two?" Celia said, as Clem rolled Madge past the Matthew's Hallmark store in the direction of the food court. "Isn't that sweet?" The woman at her cash register turned and smiled.

"Like two love birds," the customer cooed. "Look how devoted he is. Why, he looks like he could use a cane himself. I hope I have someone to look after me like that when I'm old and out of it."

"Out of it" pretty much described Madge. She was commenting on the dress and looks of everyone they passed by—and not bothering to keep her voice low. Jaw set, Clem just kept on pushing her relentlessly toward the food court end. When he reached the point where the center court narrowed for the run toward Macy's and the cutoff to the right to the food court, he stopped and parked Madge beside a bench, facing a dry fountain.

"I believe I'd like to be turned lookin' over to that Christopher and Banks dress shop, Clem."

Clem looked down at her but didn't say anything immediately. He looked like he was fixing to speak but then clamped his mouth shut. But there was a little flare in his eyes, and he left Madge where he'd put her, facing back toward where they'd come from.

Madge's own eyes flashed anger for a nanosecond, but then she switched to a mischievous grin. "The dress was blue, ya know. I just remembered that Hazel told me she'd ironed that dress special for the dance."

Clem puffed up and clinched his fist, but then he deflated—just like a balloon with a slow leak, hissing sound and all.

"I'm going to the men's room in the food court," he said in a small, faraway voice.

"I think it's that way," Madge said. She waved off toward the western corridor, but her hand swung around in the motion and fluttered toward the southern end where it ran into the front door of Sears.

"I know where it is."

Clem turned around and started off north, toward the direction they'd been headed in.

Madge turned her head and spoke into his wake. "If you pass by a drug store, a bottle of Prell is what I need. And maybe a box of those Russell Stover's chocolates—the assorteds. That's what Molly always likes to get."

There might have been a grunted sound as Clem walked away. And then again there might not have been.

Sometime later—it might have been twenty minutes, but then again it might have been an hour—Cecilia looked out of the window of the Hallmark store and saw that the woman in the wheelchair was still sitting there, facing the fountain. She was looking at her nails as if it was the first time she realized she had fingers and was talking to herself—and greeting everyone as they passed by, like she was some sort of welcome wagon or something, like she was the mall's Miss Information.

A customer walked into the Hallmark store, and Cecilia turned around to help her. Another customer followed, and Cecilia was as busy there for a while as she'd likely be in a shift.

Her shift was almost over when she glanced out of the window again, past the departing back of a customer— and saw that the woman in the wheelchair was still sitting out in the center court area.

Concerned, Cecilia went out of the door behind the customer and walked briskly over to the fountain.

"You OK, honey?" she asked, as she leaned down toward the wheelchair.

Madge looked up at her with a somewhat glazed expression, but she was smiling a little smile and humming to herself.

"I said are you OK, honey?" Cecilia repeated. "Your husband not back yet? Would you like me to find someone to go looking for him for you?"

"No, thanks, everything's fine. But, say, when Clem walked off," Madge asked in a faraway voice, "did cha happen to catch who got the last word?"

Overdue

I don't think I'd ever seen a woman who looked as tense as the one who bustled up to my desk at the Staunton, Virginia, public library with those five books under her arm.

"I hope there isn't going to be any trouble over these overdue books," she said in a "don't even think of hassling me" voice. She slapped the books down on the desk and stuck her chin out.

"Oh, I'm sure there isn't," I responded. But when I looked at the date on the first book, I let out a little gasp. "Why, this book was due in 1978. I don't understand, Mrs. . . ."

"Strand, *Ms.* Margaret Strand. These aren't my books. I don't even live in Staunton. I'm just here for a few days going through my father's belongings. He died, and there wasn't anyone else to clean up after him."

"Oh, I'm sorry," I said, as I fished around under the counter for the oldest box of overdue slips.

"Don't bother," Ms. Strand fired back loud enough that I surveyed the library to ensure that none of the patrons had been disturbed. Then in a more quiet but even more intense tone, she said, "I'm not the least bit sorry. I didn't know him. My parents split up when I was in kindergarten. My mother and I moved to Richmond, which I don't think is all that far away. But my father never even attempted to contact me after that. I sent him some letters for the first few years, but he never bothered to answer them. I just want to get finished here and get back to Richmond. I should have known he'd leave everything for me to clean up like he did with these old library books. Mom always said he didn't know how to do anything but cause trouble. Am I going to have to pay a fine or something?"

Ms. Strand was staring at me like she just dared me to say she'd be charged anything or to offer any words in defense of her father.

"Oh, no, I'm sure not," I answered. "I can't even find any of these books in the overdue file. They seem to have been taken out over a long time, but not recently. In fact, none since the late 1980s." I felt at a loss. This was the first such problem I had encountered, and Mrs. Taggert was on her lunch break.

"I'll tell you what," I said. "I'm sure we'll just forgive any fines on these, but that's really for the head librarian to say, and she's out to lunch. Could you leave your phone number, and I'll call you back?"

"Oh, I suppose so." Both her face and her tone were sour, and she let out a sigh that was sure to have been calculated to get across how much of an unnecessary hassle this was. She started digging in the large straw purse dangling from her shoulder. "His number is in here somewhere. That's where I'm staying. Oh, here it is. But, mind you, I'll be gone by tomorrow noon. I can't wait to get all of this over with."

Ms. Strand's belligerence had flustered me so much that I had failed to look the books over before she sailed out of the library. After I had done so and talked with Mrs. Taggert, I knew I'd just have to steel myself and make that dreaded telephone call. I just didn't know how I was going to put this tactfully.

"Yes, hello?"

She still sounded mad at the world.

"Ms. Strand? This is Angela from the library."

No response.

"We talked earlier today. About the overdue library books."

"Yes, I know. What about them? I didn't check them out. My father did and he's dead and not writing any more checks."

"Well, there will be no overdue charge, of course. But did you look inside the books before you brought them over?"

"No, I didn't. I've been too busy with cleaning out the mess he left here to be leafing through any books. You're not telling me that they're damaged and I'll have to pay for them, are you? Geez, this is getting to be just too much. I didn't check those books out. I don't even live in Staunton. Maybe I should have just tossed them out."

"Oh, no, Ms. Strand. There won't be any charge for the books at all." I swallowed hard before I went on, but she seemed so angry I wasn't sure I should even bother. However I prided myself about being conscientious with my work, so I did continue.

"Did you look at the Nancy Drew book and Elizabeth Barrett Browning's *Sonnets from the Portuguese?*"

"No, of course not," Ms. Strand snorted. "I didn't have time to look at the books. I just saw the library stamp on them. Why would my father have checked out books like that?"

"Those don't ring a bell with you?" I really wanted her to work this out for herself.

"No, why? Listen, could we hurry this up? I'm behind with the work here."

I could see this wasn't going to happen on its own, and I think she deserved to have it right between the eyes.

"OK, Ms. Strand. I'll make this as short as possible. You said when you visited the library earlier today that you had written your father some letters but he never responded, right?"

"Yes, so? He probably didn't even read them. My mother told me not to bother to try to contact him—that he wouldn't want to have anything to do with me. So what?"

"Well, the book that was due in 1981 was the Nancy Drew book. Inside that book I found a letter that had been folded so often it was falling apart at the fold seams. It was addressed to 'Daddy' from someone named Peggy— obviously a young girl—who was writing about the Nancy Drew book she was reading at the time. The Browning book also contained a well-worn letter from this Peggy and was address to 'Dad.' This book had been due in 1988 and the Peggy of this letter spoke of how much she was enjoying reading *Sonnets from the Portuguese* in her college English course. Now, does this mean anything to you?"

Silence. There was prolonged silence at the other end of the line, although I knew she was still on the line because I could hear ragged breathing.

Then finally she spoke. "I'm not sure I understand."

I was becoming a little choked up at this point myself. "It seems to me that he must have checked out the books you told him you were enjoying and was reading them along with you. Maybe he thought he'd be closer to you this way."

"No." It was almost a wail. But she gained control of herself. "No, that doesn't make any sense. He could have simply answered the letters."

"Maybe not," I replied quietly. "The book with the earliest due date was a children's book. One of the Baber series. You know, the ones where the characters are imperial elephants?"

"Baber? Those were my favorite books when I was a child."

"I sort of figured that out, Ms. Strand. There was something in that book, too."

No response, so I forged ahead.

"It was a legal document—a restraining order ordering a Philip Maslow not to have any contact with a Mrs. Joyce Strand and her daughter, Margaret. I take it your mother didn't keep your father's name?"

"Oh, Daddy," Ms. Strand moaned.

She didn't say anything else for so long that I wasn't sure she was still on the line. My hand started to cramp from gripping the receiver tightly, but I was suspended in time and couldn't loosen my hold.

"Miss, are you still there?" The voice was subdued and it sounded like she was crying.

My grip on the receiver relaxed as I answered. "Yes, of course I am. I guess you'd like to have these letters, wouldn't you? But we're about to close and tomorrow's Sunday. Can I bring them by on my way home today? What's the address of your father's house?"

When she answered, her voice was soft. "Oh, no, thank you. Thank you so much for calling. I'll be by for them on Monday. I think I'll change my travel plans and stay

167

around here and look through my dad's things a little more closely. Oh, and if you don't need those books back on the shelf after all these years, could I buy them?"

Bill-'N-Bob

Bill and Bob were virtually inseparable right up until good luck struck. The two had been unlikely best friends since they'd attended Staunton, Virginia's, Robert E. Lee High School together. Bill's sandy-colored hair; tall, thin stature; and love for making bets on everything imaginable was offset by Bob's dark, close-to-the-ground, pudgy appearance and puritanical pursing of lips whenever Bill launched into an "I'll bet you . . ." challenge. Of course, Bob never let Bill finish that sentence in his presence, but Bill never held that against him.

The two suffered the good-natured Mutt and Jeff comparisons of their classmates with bright smiles, and neither showed ire when they were jointly elected "Most Likely to Become Siamese Twins" at the end of their senior year at Robert E. Lee. While others in their class wandered away from Staunton to join the service, enroll in college, or drift into new lives east beyond the shadow of the Blue Ridge Mountains, Bill and Bob took their own shared path. They even married, in a joint ceremony, two Staunton girls who were so much alike that they could have held down the ends of a Broadway chorus line.

The two men became a fixture on the town's Beverley Street, walking to work side by side in the morning, each in his starched white coat, and taking their lunches together either on the bench outside the shop on warm days or over at Katie's luncheonette. In the evening, they strolled home side by side, Bill to 102 South Saint Clair Street and Bob to 104, while they reminisced on the day's head count.

Thanks to them, over the years Warner's Barber Shop became "the place to go" in Staunton to get your ears lowered and your questions about the peccadilloes of anyone in town satisfied. The two cut hair at adjacent chairs and, together, put on a show that amazed and amused all of the men of the town—and a good number of the short-haired women as well. The two were always in a good mood and never took long to learn their clients' names, the locations of the moles on their heads, and how to get to their funny bones. From morning to night Bill and Bob maintained a running tag team comedy show in which Bill never started a joke or sentence and Bob never ended one. The two became such a town institution that the Staunton *News Leader* declared in its Fourth of July editorial that contentment within the community was embodied in the word "Bill-'N-Bob."

Then one day in late autumn disaster made its appearance. Bob didn't even know that Bill was still following his vice—indeed there didn't seem to be an opportunity to do so, because the two were always so in step with each other that one wouldn't sneeze without the other one flipping out a *Gesundheit*. But that day in autumn Bill won the state lottery. Big time. And it went right to his head.

The very morning Bill got the word of the win tragedy struck. He hung his white coat on the mayor's nose as the two crossed paths at the barber shop door, and leaving the Tuggle boy with half a crew cut and without so much as a word of good-bye to anybody, including Bob, Bill was gone. Bob's lunch sack, the contents untouched, dragged mournfully near the ground as he trudged back to 104 South Saint Clair Street that evening. He arrived just in time to see the moving van back out of the driveway of 102.

Bill and his wife had, in fact, remembered to write a note to their neighbors before they left, announcing they were moving over to a mansion on Church Street right after they returned from a Mediterranean cruise—and they even included the adjoining-cabin cruise tickets they had obtained for Bob and his wife. But somehow they had forgotten to take the note next door before they left, and it had been left on the kitchen counter in the now-empty house.

Bill and his wife had been surprised and a little more than hurt when Bob and his wife failed to show up for the cruise. Bill remembered Bob's attitude toward gambling and chalked Bob's snub up to jealousy, disapproval, and a mean streak Bill had never seen in his best friend before.

More than once after they had returned to Staunton and taken up residence on Church Street, Bill's wife thought about inviting Bob and his wife to one of their barbecues, but she just never carried through. She knew that Bob and his wife just wouldn't be comfortable with their new set of friends. Truth be known, it was becoming increasingly harder to make Bill comfortable with their new set of friends either. He was walking around in a blue funk most of the time and buying every new toy in sight to fill in the time and to try to develop an interest in anything. His whole life up to that point had been dedicated to barbering—and to playing off Bob.

For Bob and his wife's part, they quite clearly knew how it was when people—no matter how well you thought you knew them—suddenly got rich and decided they were too good for you. *They* certainly wouldn't embarrass themselves by calling Bill and his wife.

Months dragged into the summer, and Bob's despondency had turned into a petulance that wasn't at all good for business at Warner's Barber Shop. There even was some talk of letting him go because his sour attitude was scaring away what had once been faithful customers. Business had become so slow that Bill's chair had been left vacant. This didn't help matters at all. During the early months following Bill's departure, Bob would get so busy that he forgot and would start up one of his jokes. He'd stop in mid joke and a prolonged silence would follow. Bob would have to look over at Bill's chair to remember that he wasn't there to finish the joke.

Now Bob no longer looked at Bill's chair at all; he just gave a heavy sigh from time to time during what was becoming an increasingly sporadic appearance of a variety of heads that needed to be cut. Bob didn't even look too closely at the heads anymore. He just sighed and clipped—and sometimes apologized halfheartedly when ears were nipped from inattention.

Thus it was that one day Bob found what seemed to be a familiar head in his chair. At first he didn't pay it any mind, but it increasingly dawned on him that this man had a

171

little gray streak right where Bill had one and that that pesky cowlick was just the same as Bill's. Just as it hit him that this *was* Bill's head in his chair, his former friend said in a pretty bad attempt at an English gentleman's accent, "Well, if you will not be so kind as to start a joke, how can you expect me to finish it?"

The barbershop erupted in relieved laughter, and Bob turned beet red. Of all the humiliation. Not only had he been dumped by someone he had counted as his best friend, but now Bill had the gall to come in here and treat him like the downstairs maid. And everyone was laughing at him.

This time it was Bob's turn to rip off his coat and head for the door—this time the one at the back of the shop—leaving in his wake a bewildered mayor who had just been called to one of the other chairs and who once again found himself stumbling around and trying to pull a starched white jacket off his head.

The head barber was just two steps behind Bob as he exploded into the break room at the rear of the shop.

"Hey, Bob. Wait up. Whatcha do that for?"

"They laughed at me. *You* laughed too. I guess you think it's real funny to see that two-faced gambler lording it over me. He ain't rich because he's better than me—or anyone else. He's rich because he showed up at a convenience store counter at the right time to buy a winning lottery ticket."

"Now hold on, Bob. Bill wasn't making fun of you. He was trying to make up with you."

"Bull."

"No, not bull. Bill. Your friend, Bill. What do you think he was doing in here today?"

"Isn't it obvious? He came in here just to make fun of me."

"Wrong. You are so wrong, Bob. He came in here today to ask me for his old job back. He found that being rich and hobnobbing with those folks on Church Street wasn't half as good as the life he'd left behind at the barber shop. He said he wanted his old chair back—the one right next to yours."

172

Silence

"I ain't playing with you, Bob. Those were his very words. He just sat in your chair to start the good times rolling again."

Bob was out of the back room in a flash. He looked wildly around the shop but couldn't see Bill anywhere. The mayor smiled wanly and pointed to the door to the sidewalk.

Bob saw Bill hunched over on the bench in the park. He knew it was him because of that gray streak and the cowlick with a mind of its own. Bob never forgot a head of hair; no two were alike. He sat down next to his old friend and tried to think of something to say.

"You know, Bill . . ."

". . . that it's going to be awful hard for me to go to the dance tonight with this half-done haircut. Everyone's gonna want to know what barber did this to me."

"Well, come on back to the shop, then, and I'll finish the job."

"Can't do that," Bob answered. "Something else I need to do first."

"What's that? Go on another cruise?"

"Nope. I'm not going to let you finish my hair until I've done yours—and showed you how a real barber works. Oh, and, Bob?"

"What?"

"Has anyone moved into 102 yet?"

"Nope."

"Good. The folks on Church Street are just a bit too snooty for me."

Last Treasures

"Ruth, what are you fingering those gawdawful things for? Look over here. Isn't that the bell tree you gave Gran some years back? Do you want it back? If not, I'm sure Dot would like it."

Ruth hadn't even realized that she was handling the two pieces of gnarled wood that had been sitting on the dresser top. Her eyes were riveted on the two gold rings that lay in front of them.

She knew. Gran knew when we visited her in this Waynesboro nursing home just a few weeks ago. She had said they just wanted to do some tests, but she knew. Otherwise she'd never have left those rings behind when they took her to the hospital. Although, with the marriage she must have had, I have no idea why she would cling to those rings so. It was a family legend that she never took those rings off. Why couldn't she tell us that day? I would have stayed longer with her then—asked her more questions—if I'd had any idea it might be our last visit.

Ruth could feel the bile rise at the back of her throat, and she found she was mad at her grandmother—but she couldn't understand why.

"Ruth, Ruth. We've only got a few minutes here before we have to be over at the funeral parlor."

"What?" Ruth tore her eyes away from the rings and turned to search the room to locate her aunt through a film of tears. Such a small room and so few things of her grandmother's left. *How does one cut one's possessions down as they are forced into ever-smaller spaces over the years?* Visions of the big, square, white house on the comfortable street in Lexington entered Ruth's head only to cut away to this Spartan little room in the Waynesboro nursing home. It always had seemed that Gran's life was connected with Lexington and that house. How was it that she ended up in this alien town—nice enough, of course—but alien to Gran other than that Cecelia lived here. What did Waynesboro have to do with the life

Gran had led? It was just a final stop. When asked why Gran was being buried here, her aunt had just shrugged and said this was where we had burial plots. Waynesboro, of course, was where her aunt lived.

But where was Granddad buried? Should Gran be buried beside him? Ruth realized she didn't know where her grandfather was buried. She knew so little about her grandfather—and she remembered nothing pleasant about him.

"Ruth Adams! What about this tree?"

Cecelia Adams, standing at the foot of the single bed, in the corner of the room, had reached into a wooden corner shelf, had turned back to her niece, and was waving a small copper wire tree with dusty brass bells with tiny jade leaves as clappers that tinkled as they jangled against each other.

Ruth mumbled something, her aunt and mother taking on hazy shapes as tears reformed in her eyes.

"Ruthie," her mother said. "Your Aunt Cecelia asked you about the bell tree."

"Yes, of course, Aunt Cecelia. Do take it and give it to Dot. I don't want it. I have several of my own."

"Well, I'm sure you'll want *something* to remember your grandmother by," Cecelia said through pursed lips. "Not those photographs over there, of course. I'm the oldest, so it's only right that those go down through my line."

"Ruthie, do you see anything you want? They said we could only be in here for a half hour and take a few little sentimental things—that most of it would go to their second-hand shop to support their programs here." Ruth's mother, Pamela, drifted over to the closet. "I wonder where she kept her afghans. Maybe in here. They'd be worth a lot of money. So, did you find anything yet, Ruthie? Ruthie? Ruthie? Now where'd she go?"

"Let her go, Pam?" Cecelia said. "We don't have much time left here. Look, there are her wedding rings. They should go down the direct line, don't you think? My Donald should get those—oldest boy in the line."

Ruth made it into the hallway before her knees began to buckle. Thankfully, there was a settee just outside her

175

grandmother's door. Tears streamed down her face. Why was she so disturbed that her grandmother hadn't told them she was so ill the last time they visited? Ruth had so much she had wanted to ask her grandmother, but she had waited until it was too late. Her aunt came to the door.

"Ruth, what are you sitting out here for? And why are you looking so mopey? Land, child, Gran was almost a hundred. It isn't as if this was unexpected. And what do you have those old wood things for? Put those down and come choose something valuable as a keepsake."

"Cecelia, come look at these." The muffled voice of Ruth's mother wafted from her grandmother's room. "These dresses look like they've hardly been worn. And they're a style much too young for Gran. She probably never wore them herself. What size is Dot?"

When she was alone again, Ruth shuddered. She felt like they were a pack of vultures. Why didn't her mother and aunt feel that way too? Of course, this was the first close family loss Ruth could remember. Maybe one got accustomed to this. She hoped not. Ruth looked down at her lap. *Now, where did these come from?* Then she remembered. The two pieces of gnarled wood had been standing on her grandmother's dresser, just in back of the gold rings. She had picked them up just before spying the rings and had kept such a tight grip on them that her knuckles were white.

Why would Gran have kept these through all her downsizing moves? There were pretty ugly, really, and Gran had had very good taste. Ruth turned the wooden objects over in her lap. Two smooth pieces of thick, twisted wood, the knots of some hardwood tree, neither more than eight inches long. They had been sitting up on the dresser on their ends at nearly an upright position. Now that she thought about it, these two pieces of twisted wood had been either in the parlor on Gran's bedroom dressers in all of her previous homes—from the large colonial house in Lexington, to the cottage she'd moved into there after Granddad died, to the retirement home here in Waynesboro Aunt Cecelia had convinced her to move to.

Ruth began to look at them more closely and saw that color-headed pins had been inserted near the top of the up-stretched arm of the largest piece. *Why, it's set like eyes, red eyes. But just this one—not the smaller one.* But Ruth hadn't actually looked at the second piece closely yet to see that it didn't have eyes. When she checked, she had been right. These objects weren't really new to her. She knew these pieces of gnarled wood, now clearly appearing as two twisted, dinosaur-like animals of smooth, finely veined wood that had been polished to a high sheen in the surf of some ocean. But Gran often said she'd never left the Shenandoah Valley and Blue Ridge Mountains. She'd been nowhere near the ocean. Such a mystery.

"Ruthie, honey, are you still out here?" Pamela's voice broke into Ruth's thoughts. "We're just about to leave for the funeral. The funeral home is over on West Main, so we might have trouble finding a parking place. A lot of your grandmother's friends are coming up from Lexington. You need to pick something of your grandmother's now, or just forget it."

"Momma, what are these?" Ruth lifted the two pieces of wood for her mother to inspect.

"Why those are Mother's 'fancies.' Now, just where did you find those? I thought she'd thrown those out years ago. But, no, I guess she wouldn't have. Such an embarrassment. All those nice things she had, and she insisted on keeping those old things."

"Fancies? What do you mean fancies?"

Pamela sat down on the settee in the hallway and took one of the gnarled wood pieces in her hands. She was smiling, and Ruth noticed that the worry lines her mother had carried around ever since they had received the news of Gran's death were smoothed out.

"That card, Dad." Pamela laughed. "Dad and Mom never went far for vacations. Dad would have taken us to Washington, D.C., or the ocean, I'm sure, but Mother said she liked the valley just fine and that no vacation could be better than hiking the trails on the Blue Ridge. Just for a change, he rented a cabin on the Shenandoah River up near

Front Royal, in the shadow of the Blue Ridge, for a summer and we spent most of our time in kayaks out on the river. Dad was such a joker. He brought these up from the depths of one of the rapids in the river where they'd been bounced around so long they came out looking like this. He brought them to Mother to look at when she was trying to pin up my swim suit that had come undone. He took some of her pins and popped them into one of the pieces of polished wood and told Mother those were her birthday present. He said they were Shenandoah Fancies and were so rare that only movie stars could afford them."

"Granddad? Are we talking about the same granddad?" Ruth was stunned. "My memories of Granddad were of a big man with scratchy whiskers and a foul temper. I always felt sorry that Gran had to put up with him."

"Oh, no, Ruthie. I had no idea you thought of your granddad that way. You only knew him his last couple of years when he was so ill and had to deal with the pain. No, he and Mother were a real couple—gnarled, but polished up to a shine, and obviously a set pair. Like these wood pieces here. Dad could have afforded to get Mother almost anything she wanted for her birthday that year—and would have—but they were so playful with each other that she insisted these pieces Dad made into animal figures in her imagination were just what she wanted. For as long as he lived, she kept them out with the good bric-a-brac in the parlor, and whenever anyone visited, she'd draw their attention to her Shenandoah Fancies that only she and some Hollywood stars owned. The guests would look perplexed, and Mother and Dad would just giggle at each other through their fingers. They were quite a pair of comedians when they were together."

Ruth sat there, numb. Gran was gone, but Ruth was only now beginning to get a good picture of her—and of her grandfather as well.

Cecilia bustled up to the door, a hefty box under one arm and several dresses and a quilt over the other arm.

"Here, Pam, all you've got is that silver-backed mirror and comb set. Isn't that the one Mother said I was to have, though? Anyway, your arms aren't full. Take this tissue paper and wrap up those and whatever Ruth has picked, and let's get over to the funeral parlor. Last chance, Ruth. There must still be something of value left in there."

Cecelia and Pamela started down the hall.

"Hurry up, Ruthie, and pick out what you want. We'll be in the car."

Ruth rose and took a another look in her grandmother's room. There really wasn't anything left in there now that spoke of Gran, other than the wispy scent of perfume that was distinctly the old woman's and that had given Ruth a settled feeling whenever she came into her Gran's presence. It was a pity she couldn't hold onto that scent forever. Just a dreary, small room, with one window on the shady side of the building, a lumpy-mattress bed, her grandmother's Windsor rocking chair, and a scarred dresser. She turned and shut the door with a quiet, final click.

"I'm coming, Mom," she said to her mother's and aunt's retreating backs. "I've found just what I want. It's just what I need for my dresser. Oh, and while we're driving over to the funeral home, I want to hear more about Gran and Granddad."

She wrapped the two wooden figures—Shenandoah Fancies to her now; sort of dinosaurs with a family story attached to them—in the tissue paper, taking great care not to dislodge the pinhead eyes, buried them in the bottom of her purse, and strode with renewed purpose toward her Aunt Cecelia's car.

Second Mom

Missy had entertained second, third, and fourth thoughts about coming this evening. Things had been progressing, albeit slowly, to this point, but it hadn't been Sammy—no, she had to think of him as Nathan now, although there'd been all those years of thinking of him as Sam Junior—who had asked for this. And up to this point she hadn't pressed on moving any faster than Nathan had indicated he wanted—or taken the initiative at all, since she felt it wasn't her right to do so.

Peggy and John were such friendly and bubbly people, taking all of this in their stride, or at least pretending to do so. It was almost as if maybe they were afraid to look at the situation seriously. There was every reason for them to feel threatened by what was going on. But they'd done everything they could to make her comfortable about this—at least to her face. They'd made all of the arrangements, the motel and tickets and everything, and had driven her down here to Charlottesville's Downtown Mall, to the Southern Café, for the performance. They'd even said they'd pay for her motel room, but there's no way she'd let them do that. She wasn't destitute. None of this was about her being poor—at least not now. Of course, there had been no indication that Peggy and John were rolling in money themselves, or ever had been.

But it was damn sure they'd done what she hadn't.

She wasn't on welfare or anything. She had a good job as a receptionist in a dentist office down in Roanoke. Her daddy had scrimped and saved to send her for two years to Virginia Southern University in Buena Vista. For some reason her daddy had wanted to keep her close to home even though he didn't pay much attention to her while she was living there in the hollow in the shadow of the Blue Ridge. Buena Vista was up on top of the Blue Ridge above the western-slope Bennett's hollow her family lived in and had given their name to.

Yes, he'd given her a start with college. But then that was the rub. He wouldn't have done it if she'd done what she now knew she should have done. And he probably only did it anyway to keep her close by but also to get her out of the hollow itself where everyone knew everyone else's business. Certainly everyone had known what she and Sam had been up to.

"There, see, Missy. They've saved a table for us over there." Peggy gently took hold of Missy's arm and guided her toward the table, set among more than twenty others in a not-so-big room with a small, raised stage at the end away from the street front. The Southern Café and Music Hall was a small-venue space for comfort food and local artists and musician gigs on a side street leading into Charlottesville's pedestrian-street Downtown Mall. Missy walked to the table as if in a haze. John went over to a bar at the side to get them a round of drinks. Beer for him and Peggy and a Coke for Missy. She'd been through her too-much beer and booze phase but hadn't had a drop of it since the day she'd received that letter from . . . Nathan. She had to keep reminding herself not to think of him as Sammy. Sammy Junior. In fact, it helped now not to think of him as Sammy Junior because it always brought up the image of Sam.

"He'll be right up there on stage, playing the drums," Peggy said as she settled the two of them at the table.

"Does he know we are—I am—here and that we're sitting at this table?" Missy asked, uncertainly. She was uncertain about so much of this.

"Yes, of course. He'll see John and me right off the bat. I'll bet that the first thing he'll do is pick us out. He's been so anxious about us coming down from Northern Virginia to hear his band play."

"And he'll see me sitting here too . . . and he'll wonder . . ."

"I doubt if he'll wonder, Missy. The two of you look so much alike—that strawberry blonde hair will be a dead giveaway, I'm sure."

"He has strawberry blond hair too?" Missy asked. There was so much she didn't know about Nathan, even after

181

the letters and the two telephone calls. So much that Peggy and John knew about him that she didn't. So many lost years. But whose damn fault is that? she asked herself.

"Oh, he hasn't sent you a photo yet? You haven't exchanged photographs?"

"No," Missy said, her voice sad. She so much wanted to know what he looked like. She'd wanted to ask him for a photo immediately—had wanted him to ask for a photo of her. She knew she still looked good. She was only thirty-six. But he hadn't done either, and she was trying to be careful about letting him set the pace of this. She hadn't gone looking for him, although she'd been plagued on a daily basis for the over twenty years it had been, about where he was, what he was doing—how he was doing. And whether he had found a mother and father worthy of raising him. Well, it hadn't taken her long to decide that he had found that in Peggy and John.

They weren't from here. They lived up in Northern Virginia somewhere and both had jobs with the federal government—probably good jobs from the way they dressed and the car they drove. They were in Charlottesville tonight because Nathan was in graduate school here at the University of Virginia—studying to be an architect, they'd said. Her daddy would have liked that. He had been an electrician down in the Lexington area, in the Shenandoah Valley, east of the hollow they lived in. He'd always said he wanted to build houses.

Sam had built on houses. He'd been a carpenter and no doubt would have moved up in that trade. He would have liked to know Sammy Junior was designing houses like the ones he worked on.

They were here tonight because Nathan was the drummer in a local band as well as going to college. Graduate school. Imagine that, Missy thought. Her Sammy in graduate school. Nothing like that would have happened if they'd stayed in Bennett's Hollow, she bet.

No, it was a good thing—the best thing—what had happened. The best for . . . Nathan . . . at least. And that was all that mattered.

182

But, no it wasn't all that mattered, Missy thought, tears coming to her eyes that she was grateful didn't show in the dim lighting of the hall. What had mattered more was that he'd found her, reached out to her—had sent that first letter. And then had answered the one she'd sent in reply, the one she'd agonized over, not making any self-serving excuses, not wanting him to just walk away in disgust after having made initial contact. Not knowing how to maneuver the shoals of that first contact. But somehow what she'd written hadn't broken the slender cord. And he hadn't asked her any whys— had only wanted to know the who.

That wasn't all that unusual she'd learned when she'd gone to her pastor about Nathan reaching out to her. Apparently a lot of young people his age reached out to try to fill in their past. It had been the pastor who counseled her to let Nathan take the initiatives in whatever was to be.

"Well, we'll have to rectify that. I'm sure Nathan just hasn't thought about it yet."

"What?" Missy asked, having spun her thoughts away and returned to the table in the dimly lit hall.

"Photos. You'll want to exchange photos. He's a handsome young man. You'd know he didn't come from either John's or my family. None of us that tall and good looking. None with the strawberry-blond hair. So much like you. You're so pretty. And you look far too young to have had any children old enough to be in college. Any children at home back in Roanoke?"

Any children? Missy thought, the ache in her heart twisting like a knife. This generous, open-hearted woman. She'd been the only mother Nathan had known all of his life. How could I intrude on her rights to him?

"No, no children," she answered, not feeling any right to claim even a sliver of Nathan. "I never married." How could she say that Sam hadn't been just a fling—at least not for her—and that there never could be another in her life that way? Her daddy had said she was too young for it to have been real and her mother had done what she always did—she gave a helpless look and retired to her bed. But it didn't matter if she'd only been fifteen. It had been as real as it was going to get.

And as far as being pretty and young looking, where the hell had that gotten her?

* * * *

Sam was nineteen. Already out of high school and gone directly into trade. He didn't have ambition higher than that. A local high school hero with strong good looks, muscular body, and a sunny disposition, he'd been everyone's best friend and every high school girl's heart throb. He was sitting pretty in life without going anywhere else or building up any more of a life than he had. Missy, fifteen at the time, had swooned over him along with all of the rest of the girls.

But it had been Missy who had caught Sam's eye and who he wooed. He wasn't the type of guy to notch his belt with conquests and brag about it, but he wasn't completely inexperienced either—and certainly not uninterested. That didn't mean he was smart enough about sex to use protection consistently, though, and Missy had been a complete neophyte. She'd been so smitten by him that she didn't—and wouldn't have—questioned anything he did or wanted to do.

From the fall of 1993 into that winter, they "did it"— at first in glens in the Blue Ridge Mountains, reached from parking areas on the Blue Ridge Parkway, on mossy and fern-cushioned ground surrounded by trees changing their colors in brilliant array, and then, when it turned cold, in the cramped backseat of his old cab-and-a-half pickup in whatever lover's lane he could find. They'd never slept together in a proper bed or without the fear of suddenly being discovered.

That hadn't stopped Missy from getting pregnant.

When she knew it for sure, she called him at his parents' home up in Buena Vista and told him he needed to come down to the hollow—that she had something she needed to tell him. Missy's family was a cold one, with a timid, sickly mother and a father who, as possessive as he was, only had time for sons. Her brothers ignored her entirely. She couldn't seek being in a real family fast enough. She and Sam had already talked of marrying and even had woven the life they would have in flights of fancy. He made good money as a carpenter already—or they at least thought he did—and everywhere he went while working, he'd keep his eye out for cabins they could rent to buy. And later, after they'd done it in the backseat of the pickup and were cooling down, he'd tell her about the cabins he'd seen and they'd speculate on how they could be fixed up. He gave her the first glimmer of what being in a loving family could be like. The stumbling block, of course, was that Missy was only fifteen, and her parents were strict as well as distant.

Of course, now that Missy was pregnant, her parents would have to come around to the idea. First she'd have to talk to Sam about it, though, and make sure he'd stand by her.

She would never know if he would have stood by her or not. He came careening down the mountain in the snow in that pickup of his, headed for her and the hollow, not knowing what she had to urgently discuss with him, and had slid off the road and down into the trees. He had died instantly in the crash.

Missy couldn't hide her condition from her folks for long. There was no question of her not carrying the baby to term. Her family was seriously religious. Her father gave her two choices. He could find a husband for her among the young men whose families lived in the hollow—she was a beautiful girl and known to be sweet tempered and the women of her family were known to breed well—or she could give the baby up, he'd give her enough college to be employable, and she could have a life of her own.

Missy wanted to think that the choice she made was because there never could be a man for her like Sam and she couldn't conceive that any man her father gave her to would be good to a child that wasn't his own. But she never stopped agonizing if she'd made the right choice. Maybe it had been selfishness that sent her to college up at Buena Vista after she'd stayed with an aunt up in Fairfax Virginia, in the Washington, D.C., suburbs until she'd had the baby—Sam Junior—and had given him for adoption up in Northern

Virginia. Numb and in shock at the time, she'd returned to Bennett's Hollow and, eventually, to the college in Buena Vista. Ultimately, because the memories were too much for her in the hollow and because her mother had died, increasingly causing her father to look to her to take up the slack in the home, she'd broken away and moved on to Roanoke.

In Roanoke, although she had many acquaintances, she had few friends—none to substitute for the family she craved—and she lived alone.

* * * *

She had given him up to have a life of her own. Missy looked over at Peggy as John returned, set the drinks down, and sat down beside her. Peggy had been there to give Nathan what Missy hadn't given him. She's the one who deserved to be here, not Missy. Missy started to rise from the table. "I can't. I really have no right—"

"Look, the lights are coming up on the stage area," John said. "They're about to go on. I think you're going to like this, Missy. He's really very good, and the rest of the band isn't so bad, either."

She collapsed back into the chair and, not being able to help herself, let her eyes scan the stage in a panic as young men streamed onto it. She could hardly make out any of the figures because she was viewing the stage through tear-filled eyes. But then, of course, there he was—the distinctive strawberry blond hair. He was beautiful. He was Sam—her Sam—in every way. Her heart puffed up until she thought it would burst.

Again she was clutched with the thought of being an interloper, an intruder into this family's happy moment. But then, settling behind the drum set and scanning the room to pick out his parents and having seen them and given a smile, Nathan saw Missy. There was a moment of confusion, then recognition who she had to be, and the smile broadened.

The smile was spontaneous, genuine. It was his father's smile.

Wild horses couldn't have pulled her out of the music hall then. She sat, mesmerized and totally absorbed, watching his every movement, lost in the merging of her past and present, oblivious to the sound. He could have been playing an accordion off key and she'd have been no less lost to the beauty and grace of him. She melted each time he looked out into the audience, caught her eye, and smiled.

When it was over and the band was disappearing through the door backstage through which they'd entered, John spoke up. "Wasn't that terrific?"

Missy looked at him, glassy eyed, still lost in the moment. Then, embarrassed, she said, "Thank you for bringing me here, letting me see him. Now, I'll find my own way back to the motel and let you three—"

"Nonsense," John said, with a snort. "Another band is coming on, but we can go backstage and see Nathan now."

"I couldn't possibly . . . he hasn't . . . ." Missy looked to Peggy, Nathan's mother, for help. She would understand. Thus far Nathan had dictated everything. He'd written and telephoned her. He hadn't sent a photo or asked to see her yet, though. He couldn't really want . . . at least not yet. She just couldn't push him on this. She had no right.

"Come backstage with us," Peggy said gently. "I saw the way he smiled at you from the stage. That's all I need to know that he's ready."

"But I have no right. You're his mother. I have no rights in that area. Surely, it's terrible for you for him even to be reaching out to me as he has."

"Oh, Lord, Missy. I don't see this as any sort of a rejection. Nathan and I are closer—more solid—than that. I admire him for wanting to find you and reach out to you. He and I have discussed this. He's not rejecting his world. He wants to broaden it—send it out to its natural boundaries. There's no rejection of me or John that I see in the boy. He doesn't need a mother to change his diapers or wipe his nose anymore. He needs another kind of mother. He himself told me that he'd be the luckiest guy alive to be able to say he had two mothers."

"But . . . but . . . how will I be introduced to him? What should he call me? I had him first, but I have no right—"

"How about what he's called you in talking to us about you since he was able to find out who you were? How about just being 'Second Mom'? How does that sound? I kinda liked it. It doesn't supplant me; it adds someone I can share this fine boy with and who can love him as deeply as I do."

As she struggled up from the table for that long, momentous walk backstage, Missy had to admit that that sounded just fine to her too. She had grieved and felt all alone far too long. A second mom would be part of the family without making claims she had no right to make.

And, best of all, it was Nathan's own choice.

Awards and Credits

"Fire and Ice" took third place in the 2011 John Grisham-judged *The Hook* fiction contest.

A variation of "Bouncing Back" took second place for fiction in the 2006 state-level Virginia Writers Club prose and poetry competition and "Thanks Rosa" took first place in the 2008 Virginia Writers Club flash fiction contest.

Several of the stories placed in the annual contests of the Blue Ridge Chapter of the Virginia Writers Club: a variation of "Bouncing Back," first place, 2006; a variation of "The Photograph," third place, 2008; "Molly's Picnic Table," second place, 2012; "Joleen Finds Her Voice," first place, 2013.

"What to Do with Rusty" shared first place for fiction in the Blue Ridge Chapter of the Virginia Writers Club special winter writing contest in 2009.

Two of the short, image-inspired short stories were among three by the author that placed in the annual Writer's Eye writing competitions of the University of Virginia's Fralin Art Museum. "Converging Divergence" won third place in the University/Adult division in 2009, and a variant of "The Passing of Little Eddie" won honorable mention in the University/Adult division in 2011.

* * * *

Originals or variations of most of these stories have appeared in the author's *On the Downtown Mall* and his coauthored *(Re)Tell Me the Stories*, in *Final Flight* by Olivia Stowe (a pen name of the author), in *The Hook,* in *The Blue Ridge Anthology*, in the *WritersNet Anthology of Prose*, in the UVa Fralin art gallery's *Writer's Eye* anthology, and in the *Skyline* annual anthology. All short stories by the author appearing in anthologies the author volume edited were selected in blind-judged contests.

About the Author

Gary D. Kessler, currently in retirement in Charlottesville, Virginia, following an international career in the CIA, is a former news agency managing editor, diplomat, newspaper columnist, theater critic, movie consultant (for such movies as *The Deerhunter, The Killing Fields, Good Morning Vietnam,* and *Volunteers*), book copyeditor (for over 160 mainstream publishing house works), and publishing consultant. His former Publishingquestions.com Web site was listed as one of the 101 best publishing guides by *Writer's Digest.*

His published works under his own name include a short story collection, *On the Downtown Mall;* volume editor for the two-volume *WritersNet Anthology of Prose* and the four-volume *Blue Ridge Anthology;* coauthor, with Carol Kluz, of a publishing reference, *Finding Go! Matching Questions and Resources in Getting Published;* coauthor, with Carole Stockberger, of a Bible study, *(Re)Tell Me the Stories,* and author of a mystery novel, *What the Spider Saw.* He is the author, under the pen name Gina Drew, of six Cyprus-based espionage/international crime mystery novels and has written some twenty novellas and anthologies under the pen name of Olivia Stowe, in which name he also is volume editor for the central Virginia authors annual anthology, *Skyline.* He has won or placed in Virginia Writers Club annual contests, the UVa Fralin Art Museum's Writer's Eye prose contest, and *The HooK* short story contest. His poetry has appeared in the *Piedmont Virginian.*

Cyberworld Publishing established 2009

All of our books are available in ebook and paperback
Stephen Bush
No Regrets
My Sister's Funeral - A Murder mystery
Gina Drew
The Koniotis Mysteries Series:-each book in this six part Cyprus set series, which travels from the island's past to its future, stands alone, but they are also all connected in various ways and form the different parts of one story.
Laughter's Echo
Salted Away
Mouflon Brigade
Amathus Armageddon
Bogus Bills
Homewrecker
Robin Hillard
Archie's Antiques Mystery Puzzles
Ridgeway Murder
Gary D. Kessler
Shadow of the Blue Ridge
Olivia Stowe
All Olivia's books, except the "Bundles," are available in paperback and e-book.
Mystery Romance
Restoring the Castle
Final Flight
The Charlotte Diamond mystery series
By The Howling (Book 1)
Retired with Prejudice (Book 2)
Coast to Coast (Book 3)
An Inconvenient Death (Book 4)
What's The Point? (Book 5)
White Orchid Found (Book 6)
Curtain Call (Book 7)

Horrid Honeymoon (Book 8)
Follow the Palm (Book 9)
Fowler's Folly (Book 10
Making Room at Christmas (Seasonal Special)
Cassandra's last Spotlight (Seasonal Special)
Blessedly Cursed Christmas (Seasonal Special)
Charlotte Diamond Mysteries Bundle 1 (Books 1&2)
Charlotte Diamond Mysteries Bundle 2 (Books 3&4)
Charlotte Diamond Mysteries Bundle 3 (Books 5&6)
The Savannah Series
Chatham Square
Savannah Time
Olivia's Inspirational Christmas collections
Christmas Seconds (2011)
Spirit of Christmas (2010)
Olivia Stowe Editor
Central Virginia Writers Anthologies
Skyline 2014
Skyline 2015
Skyline 2016